I0739438

High Octane: Ignited

Rachel Cross and Ashlinn Craven

CRIMSON
ROMANCE

F+W Media, Inc.

Copyright © 2014 by Rachel Cross and Ashlinn Craven.
All rights reserved.

This book, or parts thereof, may not be reproduced in any form without permission from the publisher; exceptions are made for brief excerpts used in published reviews.

Published by
Crimson Romance
an imprint of F+W Media, Inc.
10151 Carver Road, Suite 200
Blue Ash, OH 45242. U.S.A.
www.crimsonromance.com

ISBN 10: 1-4405-8185-1
ISBN 13: 978-1-4405-8185-4
eISBN 10: 1-4405-8186-X
eISBN 13: 978-1-4405-8186-1

This is a work of fiction. Names, characters, corporations, institutions, organizations, events, or locales in this novel are either the product of the author's imagination or, if real, used fictitiously. The resemblance of any character to actual persons (living or dead) is entirely coincidental.

Cover art © iStockphoto.com/Georgijevic and 123RF/Yuriy Panyukov and 123RF/David Manno

Acknowledgments

We'd like to thank Deserè, Chris, and Kimberly. And, as always, our wonderful editor, Julie Sturgeon.

Chapter 1

He'd been catching flashes of her smooth, tanned skin all night. In a conservative sea of blacks and taupes, her dress with its low-scooped back shone vibrant as a peacock's tail. But that wasn't what caught his eye. There were plenty of beautiful women at the Le Meridien hotel. What caught his attention was the way she carried herself; she didn't glide about like a model, or vamp about like an actress. Instead her posture was ramrod straight—Queen's Guard style.

He leaned against the wall, nursing his drink and watching, as she approached the bar. She gave the bartender a smile, revealing the kind of perfectly straight, perfectly white teeth that indicated extensive orthodontia or good genes—in this crowd either was likely. He studied her lips as she mouthed her order, his gaze dropping to her fingers drumming impatiently on the mahogany bar.

A man at least twenty-five years her senior, vaguely familiar, with thick salt-and-pepper hair, sidled up and stood close enough to indicate familiarity. He laid a hand on hers, preventing her from taking the drink from the counter. Her expression darkened, her mouth twisted, and she said something—something cutting judging by the pained look that crossed his face.

She strode away, leaving the older gent gazing after her with longing. Ronan suppressed a shudder. May-December relationships still made him queasy, maybe because he was the product of one. He gave his collar a tug—he loathed these things. He'd been to sponsor events like this his entire career and it never—

"Incredible job in Budapest, Mr. Hawes. The way you managed the pits was inspired. This is Pantech-Windsor's year!"

Ronan pasted on his professional smile and turned to greet the speaker. "Cheers, mate." Some tire corporation chap if he wasn't mistaken. American. They were crawling all over Formula 1 these days, thanks to Supernova Energy Drink. They'd money to burn. Supernova had brilliant engineers and brought new sponsors and fans into the mix. In fact, they had everything but a sane driver. Maddux, their lead driver, had more luck than a man deserved and occasional flashes of brilliance, but no sense of self-preservation whatsoever. Ronan shook the American's hand, received a clap on the back in return, and continued moving through the crowd.

Speaking of the maverick Texan devil, Maddux Bates made eye contact across the room, sending him a sly grin, Vivienne on his arm. Ronan froze. He nodded back, teeth clenched, and headed in search of the peacock with the military bearing. He'd do anything to avoid contact with Vivienne McCloud. The woman who had gone straight from his bed to Maddux's two races into the season, spawning such inspired tabloid headlines as "Hey You Get Off My McCloud" and "Bates Outrates Hawes."

Teal dress was alone on the edge of the room, studying an abstract modern painting on the wall. The older man was nowhere in sight. Ronan took a sip of his Pellegrino and wandered over.

She turned her head, her gaze sharp, assessing every inch.

He stared down into her heart-shaped face. Her nose was a smidgen too tip-tilted, her mouth a shade too wide, but her eyes were clear and intelligent. The dress highlighted their not-quite-green-not-quite-blue color perfectly.

"Thoughts?" he said, indicating the painting with his drink.

She blinked at him and turned around to resume her study of it. "I'm no expert where modern art is concerned, but it looks like it might be upside down." Her husky American-accented voice sent a surge of testosterone down his spine.

He extended his hand. "Ronan Hawes." He waited for the spark of delayed recognition, a comment about his season. Nothing. Then again, this Brussels event didn't house a strictly F1 crowd.

She assessed him coolly for a half a second too long, and then extended her own for a brief, firm clasp. "Cassidy Miller." She swept a lock of wavy, dark brown hair out of her face. Only ice remained in the glass she held.

"Can I get you a drink?"

"Yes, thanks. Double bourbon on the rocks." She turned back to the painting.

"Right. Double bourbon it is then." American whisky was almost as revolting as their beer.

On his approach back, he noticed that her gaze went beyond the painting and her jaw was set, the soft curve of her mouth a rigid line.

She started when he reappeared at her side.

He handed her the bourbon.

"Thanks." Her expression smoothed back into bland. "In town for the race?"

"Yes, you?"

"Mmm hmm."

"Are you a fan?"

"Of Formula 1? Not so much. But I love NASCAR."

He pressed his lips together. Americans and their precious NASCAR. "Oh?"

"I'm with someone who loves Formula One." Her lips quirked. "So I deal."

"If you enjoy racing, you'll enjoy F1."

She tilted her head, eyes wide. "You think?" She shook her head. "Formula One is so much more about the car than the driver."

"Interesting opinion, but there's the catch—the cars don't drive themselves."

"Don't they? With all that technology, isn't F1 less … I mean, aren't the NASCAR races more of a test of the driver's capability?"

His lips curved in an insincere smile, and despite his attraction to this woman, despite Vivienne across the room, he was tempted to walk away. It had been ages since he'd had to explain his sport to a novice. He'd more trouble with people toadying up to him than with them denigrating the sport. "You shouldn't even mention NASCAR in the same breath as F1. Those guys wish they had our cars."

Her wide-eyed gaze was steady on his. "Oh?"

"Formula cars are the fastest circuit racing cars on the planet. We can max them out at 350 kilometers per hour."

Her brows lifted.

"That's 220 miles per hour to you," he said. "To reach that speed you need perfection—aerodynamics, suspension, tire design, all of it."

"So it *is* the car?"

Was she having him on? No, she seemed merely curious.

"It's everything. The team, the technology, the engineering, the driver. All of it packed up and shipped out after every race to the next Grand Prix, racing on different circuits, on city streets—it's a global sport, not just for you Americans."

"Well, maybe if you came to the United States ..."

He smiled and raised his glass. "Ah but we do. Texas built us a brand new circuit in Austin. We'll be there in November."

"Texas?" She pretended to shudder. "You race in Monaco. Why not the streets of New York or San Francisco?"

"San Francisco?" A laugh escaped him as he pictured his car on one of those hills. He stepped back, readying his departure with a polite smile.

She stayed him, laying a small, fine-boned hand on his forearm. He studied it—no rings or bracelets, her fingernails clipped short and without varnish, rather like her method of chatting up. His gaze rose.

She was grinning at him. He'd been baited.

She drained her drink, threaded her arm through his, and stole his line. "Want to get out of here, Mr. Hawes?"

Chapter 2

Cass examined him. Hot and polite—and intense. His steady look promised something, retribution for her teasing perhaps.

He was tall for a racecar driver, six feet at least. His lean, muscular body was impeccably attired in some designer tux—tailored for him no doubt, as expected of the top British Formula One racer. These guys had it all: fame, fortune, females in spades. And every last one of them was a junkie who got off on adrenaline and speed. This guy had the blond, rugged good looks that had made him a star—no airbrushing required. In fact, he looked better in real life than in the papers. No wonder he'd been voted F1's hottest driver by *Geargals* magazine for the last three years. According to the article, his looks, not to mention racing skills, were attracting women to the sport in droves.

He'd just looked so bored—bored and smug, and she'd wanted to have a little fun. She deserved a little fun.

No, I don't. I don't deserve to be standing here, for my heart to continue beating.

She squelched those thoughts. He'd do for tonight. "Let's grab another drink for the road."

"Love to," he responded, never breaking eye contact.

"Terrific, meet me by that exit?" She turned on her heel and wobbled for a split second before she corrected. Hopefully he hadn't noticed. With that double on top of the jet lag, on top of the drinks to keep her calm on the flight, it was no wonder she was a bit woozy. Not woozy enough though, not if she was still thinking about things back home.

She wove her way carefully to the bar through the distinguished crowd—a mix of seasoned F1 internationals and local Flemings and Walloons—ordered another drink, and stopped next to her tuxedoed father, Anderson. The dapper sixty-year-old's eyes warmed on seeing her, and he waved her into the group. She stood, pleasantly buzzed, smiling patiently through the introductions, making all the right sounds of pleasure, shaking hands with the elderly couple he was talking with. She threaded her arm through Anderson's, flashed them a brilliant smile, and tugged him a few feet away.

"I'm heading out," she said, brushing a miniscule crumb from his lapel.

He looked down, frowning. "Are you okay? I'm sorry if this was too much … "

She met his gaze evenly. "I'm fine, and I'd be even better if you stopped asking me if I'm okay constantly. I'll tell you if there's a problem." She took a sip of her drink.

She turned her cheek for a kiss and gave him one last reassuring pat on the shoulder.

"Do you have your key?"

She let out a sigh but managed to stifle her impatient retort. She really should empathize with him more. They'd seen little of each other since her childhood. His overseas job had meant short, intense visits through her teens and early twenties. He didn't know how to be around her either, so his default was to overdo the fatherly concern thing. She'd deal with it because tagging along with him was an escape from her life that she desperately needed.

Ronan was boring holes into the exposed skin on her back from the doorway. Raising the clutch under her arm in answer, she stepped away from her father and headed toward the exit. She finished the rest of her drink and put the glass on a table near the door.

"Ready?" she said, brightly.

"I'm just across the street, at the Ritz Carlton."

"Me too."

His step faltered almost imperceptibly, but he continued on to the glass doors of the lobby. She couldn't help but notice several pairs of eyes—mainly female—darting over to him and then swiveling back to her. Had she encroached on someone's territory?

She barely felt the chilly night air. The bourbon served double duty, insulating her from the cold and numbing her reservations. When was the last time she'd had a one-night stand? Couple of years. She'd had to tread carefully working in a male-dominated environment and living in a small town. The civilian helicopter world in the United States was small and renowned for gossip, and she'd be damned if she'd give them her sex life to talk about.

Not that they weren't talking about her now, right this minute, in their pilot Internet forums and at their bases, about what she'd done.

Her heart rate soared, and her breaths became shorter.

They crossed at the light, and he gave her a speculative look. "So you knew who I was?"

"I made an intelligent guess."

"An intelligent woman? I like that."

"I've followed a bit of F1." She glanced up to see if this had stroked his ego. It was too dark to tell. "I follow NASCAR on television, but my dad has been an F1 fan forever."

"And your ... " he gestured back toward the party.

Her brow wrinkled. "My ...?"

"The older gentleman, is he a race fan?"

She blinked. No way. Her lip tilted up in amusement. "Uh, yeah." Who did he think the "older gentleman" was? A lover? And he assumed she'd leave her sugar daddy at a party to go sleep with a driver? Amazingly, Ronan seemed unfazed by the idea. Well, maybe a little fazed. There had been that slight misstep when she told him they shared the hotel. Her stomach churned, though from the bourbon or his outrageous ethics, she couldn't be sure.

Jet lag and alcohol might not have been the best pairing. It added up to a foggy sensation in the elevator on the way to his room. She'd used everything else to escape from her memories, so why not try sex?

He slipped his card in the slot and pushed open the heavy door with one arm, indicating that she should precede him. She was so close, she got a whiff of whatever scent he was wearing.

"God, you smell good," she blurted out. The door clicked shut behind them. "What is that?"

Expression sheepish, he admitted, "Calvin Klein, but I'm under contract with Burberry."

She smiled. "You unfaithful swine. What's wrong with Burberry?"

"Too ... British. Reminds me of Prince Charles. I have some bottles in the bathroom if you fancy it though."

"No," she said, suddenly noticing the intensity of the inner gold ring of his irises. "You've met the prince?"

"Several hang around the circuit, but I only got within sniffing distance of my own at a ceremony for an ex-teammate. I buggered off, though, before our aftershaves clashed."

Of course he was in that league. They all were. And what did she sound like? An enthralled schoolgirl.

"I know." He reached for her hand, teasing his thumb across her knuckles, making her breath catch. "This royal chitchat is putting you off, killing the moment. Just tell me to shut up."

"No, no, it's um—" She broke off as his hand slid up her arm, sending a delicious shiver to the back of her neck. She stepped back two paces. "Mind if I raid the minibar?"

He looked surprised but recovered smoothly. "Nightcap? Pardon me for not offering. Through here."

He led her over to the bar area and extracted a bottle. "Bourbon, wasn't it? On the rocks?"

She shook her head. "Straight up is fine." She didn't need him to take a trip to the ice machine. Better to get her drink and get this over with. She studied him while he poured. He was exceedingly good-looking. Enviable bone structure, square jaw. And suave. Definitely suave. What had she expected? That he'd jump her like some hick? Even standing still, her head was swimming, and her stomach was vaguely nauseated. All those drinks on an empty stomach. She'd be comatose if she weren't careful. As if on cue, the room spun. She reached out a hand and made her way unsteadily over to the loveseat.

"All right there?" The tiniest frown appeared between his eyes, but his smile remained.

"Fine. It's the shoes, not used to heels," she mumbled. Oh God. Had she just slurred?

He carried the drink over and set it on the glass coffee table, out of reach. She leaned over to grab it, nearly pitching face first onto the table. Now he was staring at her, not amused in the slightest. "You sure you're all right?"

She waved a hand in his direction and picked up the drink, then stared into the glass as the nausea welled up. "Excuse me." She dashed for the bathroom.

• • •

Well, how about that. She was plastered. Completely and utterly bolloxed. He could've sworn she was only a bit tipsy when they left the party. And now she was here in his room. *For crying out loud, can't I even get a quickie on the road anymore?*

He was out of practice. Leaving with this American woman had provided the perfect opportunity to illustrate to everyone, including Viv and that crowd, that he had moved on. Except now he had a drunken woman on his hands, probably throwing up all over his bathroom. So much for hooking up in haste. He flipped open his laptop—may as well answer a few emails. The shower went on. Good. Maybe that would sober her up.

The water went off a few minutes later. After another thirty minutes she still hadn't emerged, and there was silence behind the closed door.

He knocked. No answer. "Hello? You all right? Cassidy?" He tried the door and found it open. She lay on the tile in front of the toilet, naked but for the thick, white towel covering her lower half, curled up the fetal position with her head cradled on her arms.

"Oh God," he muttered.

He leaned over. "Cassidy?" No response. He gave her shoulder a little shake. She murmured and tucked her legs in tighter.

He couldn't leave her nude on the cold floor. He heaved her up with a grunt. She made a moaning noise, and he carried her to the bed, flipping back the duvet with one hand before releasing her onto the sheets. She reeked of alcohol. He noted a small tattoo of a black outlined object on the inside of her ankle. Some kind of teardrop? No, a stylized helicopter.

She stirred, and he backed up a step to stare down at the unconscious woman in his bed. Now what? Let her sleep it off? Dig through her purse in hopes of finding a cell phone? Even if he could find the number of the man she'd been with at the party, he didn't need that kind of scene.

With a sigh, he undid his tie and kicked off his shoes, preparing for bed. He sat down on the edge of the mattress and let his eyes freely roam her sleeping body—delicious curves, with tautness that only came from a lifestyle as disciplined as his own. And yet, he'd witnessed all this drinking. A one-off occurrence, maybe? Had she fought with her man? She'd certainly seemed anxious to get out of there. What a shame she had to be comatose.

Hours later Ronan woke abruptly. The smoke detector in the ceiling above him flashed its red eye. A hotel. But which one? Ah, yes. Brussels. His eyes closed again, but a sound next to him made his eyes ping open again. She was still here? Maybe she wouldn't mind being awakened. He grinned as his body sparked to life; his cock swelling, he turned onto his side, sliding across the foot of cotton separating them.

She was curled up away from him, on the very edge of the bed. She made another sound, this one distressed. He froze. She mumbled something he couldn't quite catch.

"I know, *I know. God!*" she said, hoarsely.

His stomach flipped. Was she on the phone? She still sounded drunk. He sat up. If that guy was on his way up here, things could get ugly. And he avoided ugly—at all costs. But she stayed curled up on her side, mumbling, "Okay. I can see … No … I can't …. *goddamn it* … lost it … Got to put her down …"

Ronan touched her shoulder, shook it gently.

She moaned then; a long, low, pain-filled sound that made the hairs on the back of his neck stand up. He scooted over to turn on his bedside lamp, then slid back over to give her a shake, harder this time.

She rolled onto her back and her eyes sprang open. Her body recoiled from him, shock mingled with horror on her face. She put up a hand to ward him off.

"Hey. Hey, it's all right. You were just dreaming," he said, gently.

Her eyes widened and she covered her face with shaking hands. She sat up and turned her back to him. He heard two shuddering breaths, and then she stood. Before he could say anything, she made her way swiftly into the bathroom, leaving him with a glimpse of her perfectly firm, pale ass.

He sat up against the pillows. What the hell was that all about? She came out of the bathroom, dress on, avoiding his eyes and the questions in them.

"Sorry to wake you," she said, stepping through the threshold into the sitting room, shoes in hand.

He watched her grab her clutch from the desk. Without so much as a look in his direction, she walked out the door.

"Hey," he called out, but the whispered click of the door shutting was the only response.

Now he was wide-awake, and it was a few minutes past four. Terrific. He eyed the scraps of lace she'd left on the floor of the bathroom.

•••

Eight hours and three espressos later, he couldn't stop thinking about her. Her little games, the way she'd picked him up, and then that nightmare and her disappearance, not even bothering to collect her undergarments. What had she said her last name was? God, he was crap at remembering names. He texted his crew chief. "Party last night. Older American guy—know him?"

"Which one?" came the immediate reply.

"With a woman half his age."

"Christopher James, Supernova Energy. Hot blonde wife."

"Not blonde, brunette," Ronan texted in return.

"Anderson Miller, oil and gas. Daughter."

Miller. She'd said Miller. Oh, pretty damn hilarious. He'd walked right into that one, as she'd never said what the man was to her. He'd just assumed, and she'd let him.

Cassidy Miller—that was it. He pulled out his laptop and Googled her.

"Holy crap," he whispered. No wonder she had nightmares. There were few details: she'd been piloting a medical helicopter that had crashed in Arizona, killing one—a paramedic—four months ago. There were no reports on the outcome of the investigation, just a few articles naming her the pilot, and the deceased, Steve Morten.

He searched on Morten to find a website memorial with photos of a thirtyish man with a young family, and then snapped the laptop shut.

This woman and her troubles were a distraction he didn't need right now. He'd had a slow start to this season, thanks to some trouble with first his engine, then the tires. He had some ground to make up to win the championship. And win it he would. He had the best crew, the fastest car, and a decade of F1 experience. He knew the courses, his weaknesses, and knew he could win. Had to win. Before the damn rules changed yet again and sent him and his team back to square one.

The Hawes name would be synonymous with world champion this year—before his father left prison. He just needed this year to show the world he could win the title for Britain and put all those rumors to rest. He had to break free from the chains of dishonor his father had cast over his family name and his career. It never took long for some snotty journalist to drag out the skeletons from the closet, and, well, he'd put up with that shit for long enough. He had a finite number of years left, since reflexes slowed with age. Yes, that damned Maddux, barely more than a rookie, had somehow wrangled first place, but not for long.

A wet course last week in Budapest, and Maddux, who was reckless at all times and doubly so in the rain, had combined to give the American an edge. Most of the drivers had enough sense to ride the edge of fear and focus, the line between control and catastrophe, but not Maddux, or "Mad X" as the other drivers had taken to calling him. Ronan scowled. The fool had gone blasting out on the circuit seemingly intent on killing himself or someone else. And that was the crux of F1. Sure, the advancements to car safety meant they hadn't had a driver fatality on a course for years now, but make no mistake, hitting a wall at 130 kilometers per hour would still be fatal, safety measures or not. After all, the cars had more in common with jets than automobiles.

Cassidy had seemed so—normal wasn't quite the word he was looking for. Grounded, self-assured—funny. And then so drunk. He still couldn't figure that. She'd been perfectly lucid, and then— bam, slurring, stumbling, and face down on his floor. He'd have been embarrassed, too, but to scurry off without a word?

He'd never been out with a pilot before. Come to think of it, he didn't know any female pilots. And a helicopter pilot at that. Too bad about the wreck, but sometimes things happened that were outside your control, and helicopters were sketchy—they seemed to go down frequently, at least according to the news. Sounded like a reasonably exciting career. But there wasn't much in this world that could compete with his current job. Her loss; he didn't have time to obsess over a failed flirtation, intriguing though it had been.

Chapter 3

Four days after what Cass internally referred to as the Ronan disaster, she stood next to her father, drink in hand, watching the preparations for the Circuit de Spa-Francorchamps. He was down there somewhere, Ronan Hawes, adrenaline pumping, getting last-minute instruction or doing some deep breathing, listening to music—whatever it was drivers did to get ready for the race. And this was a long one; more than 300 kilometers.

"Have you spoken to your mother?"

Cass pressed her lips together. "No."

Her father cleared his throat. "I think she's worried. They both are, throw them a bone."

Last time she'd talked to her stepfather, Jim, he had leaned on her to get her butt back home and get a job before the investigation was complete. He'd argued it was her only chance of being hired after what she'd done This wasn't the first time since she'd been a spoiled teenager and he'd yanked her out of Rockmont, the exclusive New Hampshire boarding school, that she couldn't stand his advice. Jim never knew when to leave well enough alone.

Yet despite their inauspicious beginning, she'd grown to love her stepfather. And as she drew closer to him, distance pushed her further from Anderson. Her mother, Tricia, bitter about the breakup, refused to allow Cassidy to make extended visits to the United Arab Emirates or the other countries where his job took him. Anderson never failed to send cards, gifts, and child support—very generous child support. He'd even gone so far as to set up a trust for her, his only offspring, but then he could afford to be generous. His job had made him extremely wealthy. He'd made a number of efforts to reconnect with Cassidy over the years, but she'd been so caught up in college, then flight school, and finally her career, she hadn't made time for her biological father, until now.

"I give out only one bone a year," she said, meaningfully.

"Cass."

"Anderson," she replied. "Don't go there. I know you all mean well, but let me handle it." She took another sip of the amber liquid, relishing the way it burned on the way down.

She hadn't been interested in accompanying her father to all the pre-race events, qualifiers, and trials. Instead, she'd kept herself busy in Brussels's quaint tea rooms and museums while her father schmoozed his way through parties with sponsors, car companies, tire executives, and the fabulously wealthy individuals who followed the world's most expensive sport. But now race day was here, the excitement in the stands was palpable, and she couldn't wait to see what all the fuss was about. Start time was an hour away, and drops were starting to fall. Funny how everyone seemed to be expecting this, and those not already wearing rain gear pulled out brightly colored rain ponchos—no umbrellas permitted—in near unison.

She spotted Ronan then at the edge of the track, in his red and white gear, sponsor logos emblazoned on his jumpsuit. He was looking up at her box. What must he think of her? Had he figured out who her "old man" really was? Her lips curved upward.

What was that sticking out of the pocket of his safety suit? She froze. "Binoculars," she said, curtly.

Her father handed them to her wordlessly and went back to some discussion about press and promotion with another Nautilus Oil and Gas executive. Cass peered through the lens until she spotted Ronan.

There was no mistaking that particular shade of teal—and that lacy edge.

It couldn't be. She refocused the binoculars and looked again. It must be something else—no. It was the thong she'd left on his bathroom floor.

Dumbfounded, she handed the glasses back to her father and downed the rest of her drink. He hadn't seemed like the type to brag about his conquests, but there was no mistaking the implications of that.

What an asshole! And I thought a British man in the public eye would be discreet.

"What's Ronan like?" she casually asked her father when he stepped up next to her.

"Hmm?"

"Ronan Hawes," she repeated. "What kind of man is he?"

He shrugged, frowning. "They're all the same, these drivers. Competitive, intense. I know Hawes only superficially. I suppose he might be a bit brighter than some. He went to the best schools, before that business with his father—"

"What business with his father?"

"Embezzlement. No, no, some type of Ponzi scheme. Apparently he stole the life savings of a few thousand people."

"Wow."

"The son had a bit of a tough time living it down, early on. Seems his name was mud over in England. Speculation about hidden funds. As you can imagine, people weren't too happy about the idea of their life savings procuring him a spot on an F1 team."

Cass took an involuntary step back. "Is that true?"

"I doubt it. After the investigation and reparations and whatnot, there wouldn't have been enough money to buy him a seat. He came up the hard way, through the ranks—one of the most skilled in kart racing, cars, you name it. Even as a teenager he won the majority of his races."

Anderson's gaze moved down to the track. "The rumors might have hurt him with sponsorships over the years. He's not always been associated with the best teams—at least not until last year. That's when Pantech, the global software company, partnered with

Windsor Engineering. They've managed to get the best minds in the business collaborating on those Windsor cars. And Hawes has certainly popularized the sport with women." Anderson winked at her.

She gritted her teeth. Terrific. She'd left her underwear on the hotel room floor of a panty-collecting womanizer. How many people had seen them leave together? Thank God they hadn't actually had sex, though that may not matter now, not with him displaying her underwear for all and sundry. Apparently her ability to judge character had been switched into the off position by lust or booze that night, or a combination of both. She cleared her throat. "So he's got the best team this year?"

"Yes. This is the year he could win it all. He's an experienced driver, brilliant really, methodical, a good bet to win or place over the years. The other driver for Pantech-Windsor, Mitchell, is solid too, though. It's Pantech's championship to lose."

"I've never heard that, about his father." *And let's face it, I've read enough websites about him over the last two days.*

"No, it's been off the radar in recent years. But you know I've followed this sport since I was a boy—and given my job, there's not much I don't know about F1."

Cassidy felt the heat rise in her face. God, she hoped this ridiculous, disastrous encounter would also stay under the radar. Surely Ronan wouldn't want that kind of publicity?

Her hands clenched into fists. "Yes, Anderson, I know."

She'd like to use those panties to wring Ronan Hawes's neck.

• • •

Ronan flipped up the visor of his helmet. She was up in the Nautilus area with her father, no doubt. Good choice of seats. They'd have a great view of the pits, and more important, the La Source hairpin. Anderson Miller had been around the sport for years. Ronan had even had occasion to mingle with him. No wonder the man had looked familiar. And the daughter was what? Bored? Looking for a little excitement by shagging an F1 driver? There was something about her ... something that infused his thoughts more often than a failed one-night stand warranted. Maybe it was simply the contrast to Viv. Guarded wouldn't be a word he assigned to Viv. And the idea of Vivienne behind the controls of a helicopter made him shudder.

Still, he had Cassidy's souvenir. Wrong shade of blue, a few shades off his favorite color, but it just might appease the gods of good fortune. Thank heavens he hadn't chucked it out. He exhaled deeply and snapped down the visor.

Time to concentrate now. Anything could happen midway through the season, with plenty of points up for grabs. He and Maddux had shared the podium a number of times already. No one had a runaway lead, and teams were fighting for every point. Tires, engines, and fuel mixes were making headlines, and everyone was under scrutiny by the press and the public. There were huge changes coming next year. A major shakeup in the rules, so the rumor mill had it. He had no doubt the rumors were true—as soon as your team had mastered the rules and applied them to the engineering, they changed again. That was just the way F1 worked.

Pantech-Windsor's head steward, Benny, smiled down at him, chewing gum at sixty miles an hour. "Warm-up lap in two minutes. Ready for this, mate?"

"You bet. Can you make this bloody rain disappear?"

Benny's weather-beaten, old face creased into a grin. "It's Spa, what do you expect? But it's not too slippery yet. Just take it easy on the La Source, especially toward the end."

"Yeah," Ronan said, not meaning it.

"And mind you don't cut a corner in the Bus Stop chicane."

"Don't remind me." He revved up the engine and listened for Benny's inevitable final question through the headphones. "Gonna win this one, mate?"

Ronan squeezed the steering wheel through his thick gloves. "Count on it."

He always hated this formation lap, but it was necessary to warm up the tires and get traction on the track, especially on a day like this. He accelerated off when it was his turn and, when the lap was done, joined the other cars assembled on the grid. He'd qualified in first place during the trials, so he took pole position. Already a good start. He stared up at the five lights. Would there ever come a time when his heart wasn't ready to explode at this point?

A trickle of sweat started to pour down his forehead until it seeped into the padding at his cheekbone. *As if it's not wet enough.* He'd never won this course, even though Britons or Germans traditionally won it. He couldn't resist one last peek at her, still hidden behind those binoculars. Binoculars trained on him. He shoved the scrap of lace further into the pocket of his suit to be sure she didn't catch sight of it.

She pulled the binoculars away from her face and gave him a one-finger salute.

She couldn't possibly know he was looking at her. He must've made some sound of surprise into his mouthpiece.

"Mate?" Benny said. "You crackin' on us?"

"Nah," Ronan replied, pushing thoughts of her away. There was no space in his brain for anything but acceleration, steering, and braking. Every molecule in his body was poised for a life or death race to the finish. And that's all his brain could process for the next two hours as he visualized the finish line so vividly he almost thought he was dreaming when he crossed it—alone.

Bathed in sweat, heart racing, he ripped off the helmet. Fresh air whacked his face—beautiful cool, Belgian damp air. He loved it. He loved this rain; he loved this rain-sodden place. He removed his right glove with his teeth and waved to the cheering crowd. Turning toward the setting sun, he waved in the direction of stand six and the woman who'd brought him luck. Yes, it was still stuffed in his pocket, along with the smooth stone he'd found after winning his first kart race as a boy.

There was the usual clamoring around him, the whole Pantech-Windsor team, good old Benny, and the reporters not far behind. He made his way to the podium, took the champagne and squirted it with relish at Maddux, who had been hot on his tail at the finish but unable to catch up. Yes, they put on a big show of smiles for the press. No one wanted to be accused of poor sportsmanship. Maddux understood that as well as he did. He gave Maddux a particularly big man-squeeze for good measure and grinned his widest as the cameras went on a blitzkrieg. These moments made it all worthwhile—the punishing workouts, the early starts, late finishes, the air travel, jet lag, and the erratic social life.

• • •

This VIP tent was where she'd be, if she were with her father. But where the hell was she then? It was impossible to do the rounds because everyone and his dog wanted to talk to Ronan Hawes. He'd had more than his share of propositions tonight. The winners always did. But he couldn't get her out of his head.

He reached into his trousers pocket to feel the silky material and the rougher edge of lace. In the periphery of his eyesight, Vivienne appeared like a vision under the soft indigo bar lighting. She was standing, or rather, leaning, by the bar sipping her usual gin and tonic, effortlessly languorous, her beautiful honey, shoulder-length hair falling in impossibly graceful waves caressing her neck, Adoring males surrounded her, many of them from his team. Maddux was nowhere to be seen, but no doubt he'd show his face before long. Ronan's fist tightened.

He couldn't even blame Viv for dumping him. She'd made it clear she was interested in commitment from the onset, and he hadn't managed to get there. The longer they were together—going on a year—the more obvious it had become that there was something missing. She was intelligent—trained as a journalist—articulate, and best of all, extremely good with people. She put everyone in her vicinity at ease, including him. But in private? They'd never managed to do much more than skim the surface. And God help him, he hadn't known if that was his failing, hers, or theirs. So she'd ended it. But to go from his bed to Maddux's? She'd known how that would sting, and how the press would speculate and make his life hell. He'd finally developed an, intense feeling toward her: loathing.

Viv caught his eye, her face expressionless, then turned her back. He spun toward the group behind him, sure of an easy entrance into their conversation. Anything to look occupied. The press could take one look, a frown, and turn it into a melodrama.

And there was Cassidy, two feet away from him, a beacon of blue. Her eyes, bright and steady, picked up the color of the dress.

"Hello, Ronan," she acknowledged, her expression set, chin lifted. The man beside her moved to let him into the circle. It was Anderson Miller. Ronan bit back a smile. Of course he could see the genetic similarity now—the striking eyes, the wide mouth. Cassidy's elegant little nose must come from the mother though.

"Mr. Miller, nice to see you."

"Ronan. It's a shame you're not wearing our logo this year." They'd put their money behind Simons, again, to their detriment.

Ronan smiled. Clearly she hadn't mentioned anything to her dad. He turned to her. "Nice to see you again, Cassidy."

Cassidy reddened a little, and her nostrils did that flaring thing that only ever meant danger with women. What had he done now?

"Yes," she said in crisp tone, fingering the cocktail stirrer in her amber concoction of a drink. "Congrats."

"We were in stand six and had a perfect view of La Source," said Anderson. "I could hardly believe you didn't skid out the way Maddux did. You're one skillful driver, I'll give you that, my boy."

"I'd say lucky, Mr. Miller. With conditions so wet, we're thankful there wasn't an incident. I'm just glad it's behind us. Next stop—Abu Dhabi—where there's not a drop in sight."

"See you there," Anderson said.

Ronan caught her eye.

God, what was wrong with her? Why were her eyes shooting daggers? She had jumped him fair and square, and then passed out in front of the loo. He was the one who should be irritated, not her.

A reporter tried just then to grab his attention, which Ronan dealt with in twenty seconds flat. His gaze darted automatically to the bar, but Viv was gone. Good. It was impossible to relax with her around.

"So." Cassidy cleared her throat. "We're honored you could drop by. It looks like everyone wants a piece of you." She made a shooing motion with her hand.

He ignored it. "Always like this after a win. I'm just happy to have a normal conversation that doesn't involve predicting the future or dissecting my thought processes that occurred at 350 kilometers per hour when my brain was liquefying."

"I'm sure that can get tedious," Anderson said. "Now, I see you're without a drink. What will you have?"

"I'm fine thanks."

Anderson backed up a few steps. "Cass, how about you?"

She lifted her chin. "You know what I drink, Anderson."

The older man hesitated.

Apart from the genetic similarity there was nothing—no body language or verbal cues—that indicated they were in any way related.

Ronan took two steps forward until he was standing next to her. Close enough for him to smell her heady scent. Close enough for her to touch his jacket. Heat rose through him, and he cleared his throat. "It's great that you come here—as father and daughter. You don't get much of that at F1 anymore."

"Usually the girlfriend or wife, right?" Cass said, brushing up against him. A surge of lust shot through him. Singularly inappropriate with her father standing there. Probably the aftereffects of the adrenaline leaving his system.

She sidled away, hands behind her back. "Yes, I can understand your confusion." Her lips were pressed together. She vibrated with something. Tension? Anger? "So, tell me Ronan, does *your* father watch the races?"

Ronan's breath caught. He was vaguely aware of Anderson's hissed, "Cassidy," sounding for the first time like he actually might be her dad. Her face said it all—defiant, angry, and unmistakably *knowing*.

"Excuse me," he said evenly, with a nod to Anderson before he made his way over to the bar. He ordered a drink, seething. What a bitch. His hand went to his trouser pocket. Scrabbled around. Then with rising panic he checked the other pocket.

She'd taken her knickers back.

Chapter 4

Cass chuckled to herself and stowed the thong safely away in her purse. She strode twenty paces away from the VIP tent before realizing she hadn't a clue where she was going. Her objective had been to reclaim her property and get away, but now what? She glanced around the emptying stands, shadowy people in the drizzling dusk all heading in the same direction of the exit. She shivered and pulled her jacket tighter across her shoulders. Her heels were sinking into mud. Thick Belgian mud. She groaned, twisting her foot to wipe it on a tuft of grass. This would require another shopping expedition. She'd spent more on clothes and shoes in the last few weeks than she had in a decade. It was fun to try on this glamorous new persona after spending most of her life in jeans and flight suits. And thanks to the trust fund Anderson had set up for her when she turned twenty-one, she could afford it.

"What's a lady like you doing in a swamp like this?"

She spun around and faced all six feet of Ronan Hawes, who'd managed somehow to sneak up behind her. She shrugged. "Getting some fresh air."

"That wasn't very nice, you know." His expression was closed.

"Yeah? Well, displaying my underwear for all and sundry wasn't nice either. In fact, it's pretty fucked up. My father has to work with these people. He doesn't need to see evidence of my—"

"Calm down. I don't kiss and tell."

"No, you kiss and take trophies!"

"Trophies? What? No, you left them and—"

"Not on purpose, I assure you."

"No, I know, I ..." He was frowning now. "Listen, I'm sorry. I would never tell anyone." He raked a hand through his perfectly cut, perfectly thick, blond hair, and her stomach did that twisting-with-arousal thing it seemed to do around him. "No one saw them. They've been in my pocket. And there's nothing to tell anyway, is there?"

"No. Thank God."

"I need those knickers," he said, leaning closer.

"Knickers—you Brits have such quaint words for things. Panties." She lifted her head and maintained the steeliest eye contact she could manage. "No."

"Please?"

She grinned in spite of herself. "My, my. Ronan Hawes, cross-dresser. What would your sponsors say?" She leaned toward him. "But I can tell you which boutique has them if you need them so badly. Why not get some heels and go all the way?"

He shook his head. "I don't think you understand. I need them. For luck."

Her stomach pitched. "Trust me, there's nothing lucky about them, or me."

"My podium position says otherwise."

"You can't seriously think that was luck?"

He shrugged. "I had them for luck; they brought me luck. I need them for the next race. That's how it works. Why have a big discussion?"

She gaped at him. "I'm doing you a favor, Ronan. They aren't lucky."

He cocked his head. "You're a pilot, aren't you?"

The smile vanished, and she felt her expression freeze. Had he Googled her? He must have. "What's that got to do with anything?"

"And you don't believe in luck?"

"Of course not. Skill, preparation—"

"Yeah, yeah, all those things and something else, something indefinable that makes things go your way—"

"Or horribly wrong," she said softly. "But that's on the pilot, not on luck or fate or any of that nonsense."

Could he really be that superstitious? How ridiculous. It would be nice to believe that fate intervened or whatever. If only she could do the same.

She wouldn't meet his eyes.

"I'm sorry," he said.

"For what?"

"Your accident." He waved a hand. "But at least you're all right."

She blinked. A member of her crew had been killed, but at least she was all right? This guy had the sensitivity of an amoeba. What did he think he knew about it? God, she could use a drink. Or two. She looked back at the tent.

He sighed. "Here's the deal."

He was bargaining?

"Unfortunately, I have to leave for a team meeting in about five minutes and then head on to Berlin tonight for some PR activities. I don't have time to fight you for those knickers, tempting as it is—" he glanced down, "especially with all this mud. But I'll need those in Abu Dhabi. I'll let you go on the condition that you promise to give them to me before the race there."

She let out a shaky laugh. "How reasonable of you. You're really hung up on my underwear, aren't you? I could just mail you a pair and save you the bother of—"

"That won't do," he murmured, "It's this pair that has the juju."

She dug them from her purse and thrust them at him. "Far be it from me to deprive you of your juju. I don't need that on my conscience along with everything else."

She turned on her heel.

"Will I see you in Abu Dhabi?"

"Yeah. I'll be the one throwing panties onto the track," she said over her shoulder, already striding away.

"Then I'll see you there," he called after her retreating back.

She mentally rolled her eyes as she hunted through the crowds of the well-dressed scions of society in search of Anderson. Luck. She'd known pilots who wouldn't fly without one trinket or another, who wore lucky shirts to interviews. Pilots were a superstitious lot. Apparently racecar drivers were, too.

Maybe it helped, when things went so wrong, to have something outside of yourself to blame. That would be welcome right about now. Instead, her conscious mind ran endless loops of that night, countless alternate scenarios. What she should have done. What she could have done. She'd do anything to get another chance at making the emergency landing that had killed her friend and co-worker. And the nights were the worst. Her memory reenacted the crash over and over again: the shriek of rotors when they hit the ground, the gasps that turned to agonized moans in her headset, and after—

She gave her head a shake and straightened her posture.

So Ronan was superstitious. May it be a comfort to him when things went bad, if they ever did. She envied him that crutch. She spotted Anderson across the room, in his element, yukking it up with some of the other teams' sponsors—the liquor group. They were a lively lot. Liquor, not luck—that was her salvation in this godforsaken mess that had become her life.

• • •

There was no reprieve from these endless strategy meetings; not unless he was dying, or, in fact, clinically dead.

The team manager gave his usual spiel, presenting colorful graphs and charts in some snazzy statistics software he'd just procured—the statistics on every driver in the top ten, likelihood of anyone being able to beat him, their driving histories, patterns of behavior on different courses, weak points, what they had for goddamn breakfast. Ronan closed his eyes at that part, picturing Maddux and his smarmy grin. Fancy charts be damned, the wily Texan was the only contender, and they might as well just come out and say it. If only Vivienne would pop something into his energy drink.

The most likely circuits to win were presented next, as if there were some kind of mathematical formula to it all. This was what irritated Ronan most—their belief that his performance on the day was somehow predetermined. What they never seemed to get, these engineers, was that it was more like chaos theory out there on the track. Like the weather, there were too many variables to accurately predict how any team would do on any given day, on a different course, in rain or heat. And that's what made racing challenging, frustrating, and exciting.

He needed four more wins. Four more days of engineering perfection, total superhuman performance on his part, sunshine, and a splash of old-fashioned good luck. That was it. Why bang on about it when he could be out there actually doing something to help his luck? So when his turn came to make a suggestion, he turned to the head engineer, saying pointedly, "What about the new tech—that top secret legal traction control system we tested in preseason? If you could get the kinks worked out, I'm sure I could use the advantage it gave me coming out of the turns. Next year'll be too late after all the damn rule changes."

The chief engineer, Lambert, was scribbling something in his notepad and he looked up, frowning. "Let me check on that with our onsite engineers in Silverstone. I'll light a fire under them." Those in the room who remembered the fire during the testing of the new technology tittered at the unintended pun. Ronan didn't. Gregor, the test driver, had barely escaped uninjured when the damn car had ignited. And it could've been much worse. They'd shelved it after that incident, or so they'd said, but he had no doubt the engineers were still tinkering. Benny scowled at a piece of paper one of the engineers had pulled out. Ronan recognized the intent etched in his old engineer's weather-beaten face. That new hybrid system would put them well out in front if it could be made ready in time. He could count on Benny to make it happen.

Chapter 5

"Anderson? Can we go now?" Cass hollered from the sitting room where she could overlook the magnificent Abu Dhabi F1 circuit from her enormous Yas Viceroy hotel window. Beyond the circuit, desert dunes shimmered into the fast-disappearing twilight. As usual, her father needed longer to get ready than she did. What was he doing anyway? Polishing his cufflinks? She needed a drink, and she needed it now. But there was no way she was braving the locals' politely concealed stares by being so crassly Western as to go drinking alone.

The hotel itself was a far cry from the cozy floral wallpapers of the Brussels hotel where she'd spent the week before the Spa race. This place was elegant and contemporary, with unique touches, such as the flooring with racetrack-style lines in case you forgot what the main attraction of the place was. Indeed, everyone here was here for one reason only—and she was hardly going to forget *her* main attraction. Maybe he'd be at the rooftop bar? But what if he had all his cronies with him?

She stared into the mirror. Should she have gone with the red strapless? She twisted to evaluate her dress from all angles. This white number with the black trim she'd been talked into at the boutique downstairs was too—something. It wasn't her. She groaned. Of all the dumb things to be thinking about. Since when did she worry about what she was wearing? This F1 scene was doing a number on her.

Hearing a rap on the door, she walked over and threw it open. "Hello, Anderson."

"Enjoying the view?" he asked.

"Yes, I can smell the rubber burning already."

"This is the best track of all." He rubbed his fists together in obvious glee and she got a glimpse of shiny gold cufflinks in the shape of little F1 cars. "You look beautiful, honey. I'm so glad you could make it all the way out here."

"Don't have anything else to do," she said.

Anderson shot her a sharp look that she deflected with, "Let's go, I'm starving."

The shining elevator complete with an enthusiastic attendant shot up to the rooftop bar. She gasped at the view it offered over the track. In the rapidly dimming light, the space-age architecture became delightfully apparent; mind-bending organic meshes of pure light covered the hotel and a portion of the track. A quick glance around the bar assured her there were no dashing F1 drivers lounging on the tan leather looking bored. The evening crowd hadn't come in yet it seemed. A geeky looking Arab with John Lennon glasses tinkered away at a piano.

A bourbon later, the sharp edges of the world began to fray a smidgeon. But it wasn't enough, not by a long shot. While Anderson was engrossed in the menu, she beckoned for another drink. The waiter cast an inquiring eye at Anderson, and she shook her head crossly.

"Another?" Her father's eyebrows shot up.

"Anderson," Cass warned. "So, who's favored to win this thing tomorrow?"

"Oh," he grinned. "I think your friend might have a fairly good chance."

"He's not my friend."

Nice. I said that with all the sophistication of a six-year-old.

"Well, whatever he is." Anderson was laughing now.

"What makes you so sure he'll win this one?"

"Drivers like this track, and he's a dry-track kind of guy. Maddux tends to get him on the wet ones, like Spa Except last time, of course. I'd imagine he's riding a wave of good luck."

"You people and your obsession with luck. Whatever happened to skill?"

"Oh at this level, that's a given. But to win … I don't know. I've seen many races and all the circuits the world over many times, in all conditions, and I think it's a combination of what's going on in that driver's head and what the gods are thinking on the day."

"Anderson," she groaned, "I'll need another drink if you're going to get all esoteric on me. Ah … speaking of." She beamed at the impassive waiter, took the drink from his hand, and inhaled the vapors of her second bourbon.

"So how's it going?" he asked.

"How's what going?"

"Life?" Anderson shrugged. "We hardly got to talk in Belgium."

"Fine."

"Well, we'll have time to talk here. I realize there's a lot to catch up on, but what I'm concerned about are your plans, you know, for the future."

Cass prodded her ice cubes. "No idea."

"I don't expect you'll want to go back to … all that anytime soon."

She looked up sharply. "All what?"

"To being a pilot. It's a dangerous business. I mean, it's up to you, of course, but until you know the outcome of the investigation, it may be a chance to reassess priorities."

Her eyes narrowed. "Reassess priorities? Being a pilot is my life. There's nothing to reassess."

Anderson polished his silver knife with a napkin. "You've had a near-death experience, Cassidy. Surely that's got you thinking?"

Cass took a huge gulp of her drink. "Of course, it's got me thinking. You don't just walk out of a wreck and go on as if nothing happened. I had to meet with the crisis team after the accident. Talk about what happened with my employer. It's all good." She finished the drink in one swallow.

Her stomach heaved. If she couldn't bear knowing what she'd done, how could Anderson? How could anyone?

"It's all good?" he repeated, whether because the expression was foreign to him or he didn't believe it, she couldn't tell.

"This is helping." She put her empty glass down.

"Your drink is helping?" he said, a note of alarm creeping into his voice.

Oh God. She was never going to live down the state she'd been in exiting the plane. She'd been so terrified to fly, it had taken four drinks at the bar just to get on the damn jet to Abu Dhabi, and the flight hadn't been long enough to completely sober her up. Anderson had barely been able to mask his shock as she'd stumbled off the plane. Not the best country in which to be inebriated in public.

"No, I mean … all this … the F1. It's … a total thrill, and seeing this danger has anaesthetized me, in a way," she lied. "Can we talk about something else? I'm trying to move past what happened. Tell me about the course. I want to know which bends are likely to see the most jockeying for position, if that's the technical term for it."

Anderson settled into his favorite subject with relish, and she kept him talking with nods and appreciative "mmm-hmms" all the way through their exquisite three-course dinner. Until something, or rather someone, registered in the periphery of her vision, advancing rapidly.

Sure enough, when she turned her head upward it was into the smiling, tanned face of Ronan Hawes. Casual in a light blue polo shirt and jeans, he oozed class and a fatal sexiness, standing in a relaxed pose, brandishing a radioactive green longneck. From the way he glanced from her to her father, he was calculating how to talk to her alone. Or maybe that was just her wishful thinking.

"Ronan." She smiled and stood. He was near enough to get a gentle waft of that Calvin Klein aftershave again. God, she wanted him.

She edged away again, flustered, and let Anderson shake hands.

"Come join us," Anderson said.

Ronan shook his head. "I'd like that, Mr. Miller, but I really need to get to bed soon." Here his gaze wandered to her, and she darted her attention to the glasses on the table.

She bit back a grin.

Real subtle, dude.

"Need to be in top form tomorrow," he was saying.

"Oh, yes, of course, of course," Anderson said. "How long have you been in town?"

Ronan dragged a chair over and sat down beside her. "Three days. Enough to refamiliarize myself with the circuit, you know?"

Cass took a gulp of her drink. How could she get rid of her father? He wasn't the type to take a hint. She looked up again. "What's that you're drinking? It looks dangerous."

He narrowed his eyes at the bottle in his hand. "It's noxious. I'm just holding the bottle."

"Well, why not get something you'd like to drink?"

"My sponsors don't do drinks. This is Fizzbang Energy, the main rival to Maddux's Supernova. I mean, someone's got to represent the other side. Look at the sheep over there." He beckoned to the group of drivers and their teams and glamorous girls, uniformly holding orange cans of Supernova, some putting them down on the grand piano.

Cass winced. "I guess none of you can drink alcohol before a race then?"

He shrugged. "Haven't much use for it at any time, to be honest." He glanced at her drink for a fraction of a second and cleared his throat. "Have you been here long?"

"No, just got in four hours ago, and by the time we got out here from the airport and unpacked, it was time for dinner." She yawned for good measure.

"You've done well to stay awake this long." Ronan rested his arm across the back of her chair and did an easy scan of the room. He turned back to Anderson. "Oh, there's Mr. Al-Saeed, CEO of Treadhill Motors. He wanted to talk to you about a franchise, Mr. Miller."

"Oh yeah?" Anderson said, eyes twinkling in a way that made it obvious he knew Ronan's game. He pushed back his empty glass and slapped the tabletop. "Well, I'd better get over there, hadn't I?"

"No, stay, he's already on his way here." Ronan stood up and his hand grazed her shoulder, sending shockwaves throughout her body.

She stood, too. Immediately she felt a wave of curiosity emanate from the piano crowd. They were doing that looking-but-not-looking thing, spying at her in various mirrored surfaces surrounding them, assessing her, speculating.

"I'll see you at breakfast," Anderson said.

Mr. Al-Saeed came over and nodded curtly to them all.

She knew better than to offer to shake hands as a woman in a Muslim country. Though leaving a bar with a man who wasn't her husband was no doubt ten times worse. She glanced around, but the only ones seeming to be judging her were the Western F1 crowd.

"So, what have you been doing?" Ronan asked.

"Shopping, this and that."

She tossed back her drink; his eyes never left her face. The room temperature seemed to be rising, despite the high-tech air conditioning. Placing her glass carefully on the table, she caught their waiter's eye. Maybe just one more. She turned a bright smile Ronan's direction. "What were you saying?"

"Why do you drink so much?"

Her mouth opened. And closed. Opened again.

"I enjoy it."

"Bourbon?"

"Not classy enough for you? And you're drinking that nastiness? Those energy drinks are probably worse than any alcohol."

He shook his head. "Can't be."

She smiled to cover her annoyance.

"Ready?" he asked, extending a hand to help her up. She took it, wobbling to her feet.

He gave her a look.

"It's the damn heels," she muttered. "Honest to God, I'm not going for a repeat performance of my face-down-on-the-bathroom-floor routine."

He laughed. "You can't imagine how relieved I am to hear that."

She followed him to the exit doors. He plonked the bottle inside a potted palm tree and led the way to the spacious corridor at the elevators.

"My God, your subtlety with Anderson bowled me over back there," she said.

"One of my many talents." He grinned. "As is this." He cupped his hands around her neck and tilted her chin up. Her heart hammered. She was getting lost in his hazel eyes. His lips pressed down and urged her mouth to open to him. She was dizzy with need as his tongue stroked hers. His hands slid down the exposed flesh of her back, holding her to his hips, pressing against her, insistent. A shiver shook through her.

When they came up for breath, he asked, "Your room or mine?"

• • •

Ten minutes of excruciatingly polite chitchat later, Ronan finally cocked his head toward the bedroom. "So?"

It was the signal she'd been waiting for.

She stood and kicked off her shoes. Not waiting for his reaction, she slipped off her wrap, pulled the dress from her shoulders and stepped out, clad only in her cream underwear and matching lacy bra. She didn't want to think or draw this out in some striptease-type scenario. She wanted it now. She lifted her gaze from the dress on the woolen carpet.

He was watching her calmly, almost impassively, as if she were room service come to fill the minibar, but when she came closer to him, naked lust crossed his perfect features as his eyes scanned her body. He rose from the sofa, toed off his shoes, unbuttoned his cuffs, shook the cufflinks on the coffee table, and stripped off his shirt. His gaze never left her as his hands went to his belt, unbuckling, unthreading while she watched, finding it difficult to catch her breath. God help her, she was desperate. Desperate for him and nervous.

Where had her buzz gone? She'd been slightly tipsy when they'd arrived, but now her body was anything but relaxed. It was clamoring for him. He shucked his dress pants and socks, tossing them carelessly on the floor. He stood before her, his chest muscular and well defined, covered in a sparse amount of golden hair. Her attention drifted lower, taking in his cock jutting out against the thin cotton of his black boxer briefs. Then he stripped those off, too. He took two steps away from the coffee table separating them, and she shivered, her body throbbing.

Ronan yanked her lingerie-clad body against his. He put one arm under her hips and the other behind her head. He brought her to his eye level and lowered his mouth to her neck. It was electrifying. And that scent. She'd never be able to smell it again without associating it with this moment. He backed her up until she hit the wall, then he held her there with his body, panting. His chest was hot and hard against hers.

Her stomach clenched, at the mercy of the familiar and overwhelming ache of arousal. She raised her head and wrapped her arms around his neck, bringing his head down. Her lips met his again and again; she wrapped her legs around his hips.

He thrust his tongue into her mouth, ravaged her, and she moaned. This was no exploratory kiss like the one downstairs. It was hot and hard and desperate, and she was out of control. She urged him on, running her hands through his thick, soft hair. His mouth caught her breath, her hips moving restlessly, impatiently, against the hardness of his cock. The only thing separating them was the thin cotton of her now-soaked thong. She rubbed herself against him, her mouth glued to his.

His free hand popped first one breast, then the other from the confining fabric of her bra. His mouth left hers. He palmed her left breast, lifting it to his lips, sucking the peak into his mouth, hard.

"Ahh, Ronan. Condom?" she managed.

He nodded, but his mouth had moved to her other breast, doing the same pleasure-pain suck on her sensitive flesh. She moaned and locked his head to her with her arm. His hands went to her hips to grind her harder against the hot strength of his arousal, his open mouth leaving a trail of heat as it traversed her neck, her jawline.

She wrapped her legs tightly around him as he leaned away, her arms linked around his neck. He staggered away from the wall and carried her into the bedroom. Once by the bed, he grasped her arms and held them away, then her legs, depositing her on the bed. She scrambled back, pushing off pillows, thrusting the bedcovers down until she reached plush cotton sheets, lifting her hips to slide off the thong, reveling in the ache at the apex of her thighs, the insistent pulsation. She glanced up to see him watching her, his face taut with intensity and desire, holding a condom. He sure was johnny-on-the-spot with that thing.

I won't think about that ... about how many women have come before me.

Men who could get what they wanted, when they wanted, did.

Her body was protected from his past, her heart protected by her past.

Four long strides took him over to her.

Her gaze met his when he finally looked up from where he'd stroked the condom on himself.

Pushing her back on the bed, he knelt and put one of her legs on either side of his hips. She closed her eyes as his hand found her. His two fingers made slow circles on her clit, stroking, teasing. She arched her back, panting.

Her eyes opened, and he was watching her. Too intense. Too intimate. She reached for his hips, grasping them, pulling him down on her. His tongue pressed into her mouth as his cock surged into her slick opening. Her breath stuttered as he worked himself inside. Her legs went numb, and she had seconds to realize she was about to come, hard. Too soon. She tried to raise her hips, to delay her orgasm, but his were inflexible, pressing her farther into the bed, stroking slowly in and out of her swollen channel.

"No, I ..."

Desperate, she pushed against his shoulders. It was too late. She stiffened. Bucking on the bed she came with a long, hoarse cry that broke the silence in the room. She sank back panting, avoiding his eyes and covering her face with a shaking hand.

He thrust into her, tremors wracking his body.

"God, Cass."

Her mouth went dry as she watched him enter her, over and over, thick and hot against her flesh, his thrusts taking on more urgency until she felt him tense on a push that seated him all the way inside her. He came with a long, agonized groan.

It was a thousand times better than alcohol at making her forget.

Chapter 6

Ronan stood on the tarmac the following morning and stretched his arms wide, raising his face to catch the dry Abu Dhabi desert breeze—the last he'd get before sinking into his goldfish bowl. The heat would abate soon though, before they'd race tonight. Yet another reason to love this circuit.

The roar of the engines being tested last minute, the familiar, noxious addictive fuel smell, the sun beating down on the bone dry track, this was all ... home. And today, he'd win. He slid his left hand into his chest pocket. Yes, it was right there, the silk cool against his fingertips.

It had been hot. Definitely. But more than that, she held his interest when they weren't in bed. Which wasn't a novelty exactly, but he was thirty-three years old, old enough to know that sex with a hot, intelligent woman was a million times better than hot sex with a dolt. She was uninhibited in bed and quick witted out of it. And as different from Vivienne as was possible within the same species.

He shoved the underwear deeper into his pocket. She'd snuck out of his room at some point during the night, but they'd already exchanged two text messages. He needed to take care with whatever this was. It could be awkward sleeping with the daughter of another team's sponsor. Even more awkward if Pantech's financial woes left Windsor in the lurch. Rumor had it Anderson's oil and gas company was looking to be more than just a team sponsor. They were hoping to partner with a car company and race a Nautilus team in the not-too-distant future. Windsor could be that partner.

Yeah. Time to put Cass out of his head.

He pulled the stone from his pocket and threw it across the tarmac. Three bounces. Not bad. Four would've been better. But three was okay, too. He retrieved the stone and put it back in his pocket with Cass's scrap of lace.

"Hey, don't forget to kiss the ground, Hawes." Maddux had appeared suddenly, swinging his helmet, the usual cynical grin creasing his tan cheeks. "You need all the luck you can get."

Ronan shook his head. "Nah. You're standing too close, mate. It's contaminated."

"Suit yourself." Maddux slipped on his helmet. "I'm sure you'll find something to blame if you don't win, so it may as well be luck." He turned and started to strut away.

"Doing a rain dance?" Ronan called after him. "I think the forecast is clear."

Maddux turned and gave him that smug grin. This guy's range of self-expressions were limited to smug, petulant, and maniacal. He saved his look of evil triumph for whenever he actually managed to win. What did women see in him?

Maddux gave him a single-fingered salute and slapped down the visor that reflected the high sun. Disconcerting how harmless he looked with the full gear on; just like any other driver. Ronan turned toward his car.

•••

"Oh God, oh God, they're starting!" Cass screamed above the roar of the twenty-four F1 engines revving up. She grabbed the binoculars from Anderson and peered through. Ronan had waved in the direction of her stand—definitely.

She waved back.

Adrenaline coursed through her … something she'd not felt since … since … well, in a long time. This was gleeful adrenaline, not the cold dread triggered by impending death. Hopefully it would keep her awake. She hadn't slept most of the night out of fear of becoming a raving lunatic in her sleep. Eventually she'd given up on sleep and slipped out of his room.

"Cass, you're not even looking in the right direction," Anderson said. "And why are you scrunching up your face like that?"

"Oh." Speechless, she handed him back his binoculars. Yep, that's what she'd forgotten to buy in the palatial shopping mall yesterday. Binoculars. What was happening to her that she'd buy lingerie instead of vital equipment?

The flag went down. The world seemed to erupt in a cacophony of noise and movement everywhere as the cars dissipated into streaks of color, lights flashing. The crowd swayed in excitement, with some first-timers even holding their fingers to their ears. The sound here at this venue was magnified, bouncing off the smooth, broad surfaces of modern architecture, amplified to a painful level. Everything about Belgium had been quainter. This was exhilarating, blisteringly warm, impossibly over the top—utterly addictive!

"He's off to a perfect start," Anderson yelled. It was an implicit understanding between them that "he" could refer to only one driver, Anderson's way of saying he was aware the two of them had something going on. At least he wasn't going to stick his nose into her affairs. She nodded back vigorously, not taking her eyes off the track.

She couldn't wait long to grab the binoculars from him again to watch Ronan's progress in the bends. He was second place, but once the pit stops started it could all change. The leader was that orange team, his rival Maddux, and if the press were to be believed, Ronan's nemesis.

"Come on, come on," she chanted. She could shout and no one would hear her. So she tried that. "Ronaaaan," she called as his car sped around the nearest bend.

The last Doppler whine, and they were gone to another part of the track. Relative quiet was restored. Cass turned her head back to Anderson, who was watching her.

"It's good to see you happy again," he said.

"It is fun, isn't it? I can see how you'd get into this. It's more thrilling than NASCAR," she admitted.

He laughed. "High praise, indeed. Don't worry. I won't tell any of your friends back home. Not that I know them."

Cass stiffened at the mention of home.

"Oh, first pit stop already," Anderson said. "Who is it? Oh, them. Okay, we can forget about them, it looks like engine trouble. New car, too." He shook his head disapprovingly. Cass let him ramble on until Ronan was coming around again. If cars had personalities, she could swear there was animosity crackling between Ronan's red and silver one and Maddux's black and orange one just ahead. She could barely contain her own frustration, so his must be off the charts. "Oh come on, Ronan, just get in front of that asshole," she said. "You can do it, you can do it."

And then they were gone again. Cass's mind began to numb with fatigue as seven more laps passed in similar fashion. Yes, it was addictive, but it also required stamina to just stand here and be subjected to this noise, this heat, and these emotions, frustration and fear warring. These were dangerous vehicles on a potentially deadly course. All the safety standards in the world didn't change the fact that one false move could cause death or serious injury.

"Ronan's slowing down," she called to her father.

"Don't worry, it's a normal pit stop. He's due."

"Oh." She handed the binoculars back, unable to watch, unlike Anderson who was timing it on his stopwatch as if he didn't trust the fifty-foot digital clock looming over them.

"Good Lord, that was one hell of a quick tire change."

"Great!" Cass stood up to see his progress and how far behind the orange car he was. Catching up. Fifth place now, but the other four hadn't had a stop yet. She settled back on her seat and resigned herself to the relative logic of F1—positions only made sense when you knew how many stops the drivers already had. Somehow it was easier to keep this in mind with television announcers reminding you. Right here, right now, fans just wanted their driver out front.

"Oh look, now Supernova is stopping, too—that's Maddux, isn't it?" she said. "And Ronan's in third place."

"That's Maddux," Anderson agreed, absently focused on his golden stopwatch. He clicked the stopper decisively when the orange car departed from the pits again, declaring, "Ronan's got a one second lead."

Could he hold it?

"They'll need another pit stop around the sixteenth lap though. Let's see if he can keep it." They both stared at the monitor, and sure enough the name at number one was now "HWS." Short for Hawes. Cass shrieked, finally believing it. "Cool!"

By the time the second pit stops kicked in, she was an expert at counting. She'd read it should take three seconds. Best case? Two point something. And Ronan had done it again, best case. As he'd kept saying last night, this track was a favorite.

An "ahooah" from the crowd snapped her attention back to the circuit.

"What?" she almost shrieked.

"There." Anderson pointed to the curve nearest on the east side. "Ronan swerved. No idea why. But he's lost some time."

Cass stared at the monitor ... two laps left.

"He's killing it now. Look. "

She squinted to see what Anderson so plainly saw, but it was the same neck-and-neck behavior as before. No wait ... where was the orange Supernova car? She gasped when the camera moved ahead and it appeared, a good second ahead.

"What? Damn it! That's Maddux. How did he take the lead?"

Anderson put down the binoculars and gave her a genuinely consoling look.

Cass stared at her feet, wondering what must be going through Ronan's head. Her forehead was throbbing with angry frustration on his behalf. And if she felt like this, he must be apoplectic. "He really wanted this one," she said aloud.

Anderson's lips quirked. "No, Cass. They want them all. Every time. These guys don't deal well with any place other than first. Second is as bad as last."

•••

A couple brushed past them before she registered who it was—that driver, Maddux, strutting by with a gorgeous model-type on his arm. She turned her head to watch their progress through the crowd, which clamored around them. He was the same height as Ronan and nearly as attractive, but that swagger was a complete turnoff.

When she finally found Ronan, he was cornered by the coffee stand with some young journalist hounding him. He wiped his brow with a weary shift of the eyes that Cass instantly recognized.

She shoved her way through a mass of colorful jumpsuits and marched up to him.

"I'm sorry," she said in her sternest voice to the journalist, "but he's had enough interviews."

"Yes, and who are you?" inquired the reporter, instantly turning his owl-like gaze onto her.

"I'm his … life coach."

"Oh. Can I ask your name, ma'am?"

"Coach," she said. "Ready?" She smiled at Ronan, who gave her a half-hearted attempt at a grin.

"Am I ever," Ronan replied.

"Then c'mon, champ."

Ronan winced.

The owl eyes widened behind the reporter's black-rimmed glasses, and then he trotted off.

"You okay?" Cass asked.

"I've had enough of the rehash. Maybe I can sneak out." He beckoned to a catering door concealed behind a stack of alcohol and Supernova drink crates.

Cass marveled at how quickly night had fallen. She shivered a little.

"Where's your father?"

"He's with his oil crowd. They're all going to some swanky place downtown to discuss business." She shrugged. "I'm free for the night."

"You propositioning me again?"

"Do I have to?" she asked.

Ronan dragged a hand through his hair, came closer and titled up her chin with his finger. She read the fatigue in his features, but more than that, defeat. Against the backdrop of dusk, with a patch of stars twinkling around him like a halo, he was as alluring as she'd ever seen him. The tension in his jaw and forehead only amplified the effect.

"I'm going to have to beg off. I'm not good company tonight. Never am after I lose."

"No?" She took his hand. So Anderson had been right. Second was as bad as last. He and Mitchell, the other Pantech-Windsor driver, were still in contention, points-wise, for the championship, but evidently he was taking second place hard.

He exhaled and averted his gaze toward the night sky. "Please, don't be offended. I'm … I … you never get used to it. Defeat. At least I haven't. Not in all this time. I'm … if it were socially acceptable I'd go off somewhere and rage about it—howl at the moon or something." He sighed heavily. "At least, I would if I had the energy."

"We don't have to do anything. Hang out. And I won't take it personally. I'm competitive as all hell, myself," she admitted.

"Yeah? Well I'm a moody bastard when I lose. No one can stand to be around me."

"You exaggerate."

"I'm not. I pace and tear at my hair. And if you offer me platitudes, I swear I won't be responsible for my actions," he warned.

She kept a level gaze. "I would never. I'll hand things to you to throw at the walls. How does that sound?"

His face cracked into a grin. "Sounds great. Until the papers get ahold of it. They never let go of stuff like that, you know—trashing hotel rooms." He tugged her hand, leading her into the lobby, nodding at the bellhop.

But he didn't tear his hair. She put on the television and settled next to him on the king-sized bed. Such opulence—Egyptian cotton bedclothes with razor sharp edges, pillows that whooshed with airy softness, flattering diffuse lighting, original artwork on the walls, and everywhere, expensive natural materials blending in subtle harmonies. Did he even notice these finer details anymore? Or maybe he'd grown up with this degree of luxury. Her life in the States was nothing like this. She'd spent enough time at an exclusive prep school to see how the other half lived. Her friends back then were the offspring of some extremely wealthy people. She skied, knew which fork to use, which glass was for white wine and which for red. But it had been more than a decade since she'd hung out with the kind of people who could afford to go to F1 after-events and VIP parties. And it was another reminder that she didn't fit. Didn't want to fit. She loved her job and her life back home. Flying and helping people, being part of a team. It was the best of all worlds and there was nothing else like it.

• • •

Ronan started to unbutton his shirt. Cass was staring at the television, which was cycling through its explanation of the hotel amenities. He switched it off, finally getting her attention.

"Movie?" she asked.

"You."

She went to her knees on the bed, and something in her expression sent the blood stampeding from his head down to his cock. She was so damned—eager wasn't the right word. Neither was enthusiastic. Intense. That's what she was in bed. Out of it, she was reserved.

Cass stripped off her dress and unhooked her lacy bra. His mouth went dry. God. Her body was unbelievable. Compact, strong, lithe, and her breasts were perfect. Absolutely perfect. She wasn't rail thin, and he loved that.

She scooted across the bed and knelt, raising her hands over her head. "You have a thing for tits."

He grinned, shedding his pants, peeling off his socks, finally raising his gaze to her dancing blue eyes. "Your tits. Yes." He pulled a condom out of the drawer and tossed it onto the bed.

She held her breasts up for his inspection and laughed at the expression on his face.

"Cass," he groaned, lowering his head and taking her mouth in a soul-stripping kiss.

He released her mouth, gently directing her until she lay flat on her back in the middle of the bed. He peeled off the scarlet thong and spread her thighs.

"Uh," she said.

"Was that a protest?"

"Hell to the no," she whispered.

Her body was flushed from chest to forehead. Their eyes met and held. He lowered his head to the apex of her thighs. Her hands gripped his head, holding his hair almost painfully. Her body was taut as his mouth dipped to taste her. He licked into her, using one hand to still her squirming hips. He coaxed her, plying her slickness, vibrating his tongue fast, then slow on her clit, until he discovered the rhythm that sent her rocking into his mouth and gasping his name. Her body arched off the bed, and he thrust two fingers into her. She came apart with a low scream, her body clenching against his fingers. He didn't wait for the aftershocks to end. Ripping into the condom, he smoothed it on with shaking hands. God. He couldn't get inside her fast enough.

He worked his cock into her; she was so tight, her tissues still swollen from her pleasure. She raised her hips, taking him the rest of the way, and it was his turn to gasp.

"Cass," he muttered.

Her hands yanked on his hips, more, harder. He was out-of-control jackhammering into her, only vaguely aware of the headboard making a racket against the wall when she came again, crying out his name. His breath held as everything coiled inside him, and then he was coming so hard into her.

Seconds later he came back to himself enough to realize the body underneath him was shaking.

He rolled off, to his side. "Geez, sorry. Was I crushing you?"

She was trying, unsuccessfully, to hold in laughter.

"What?"

"That," she gasped, indicating the headboard. "You may have damaged the wall. And shouting? Ronan, I don't think you're going to need to throw things. The people in the next room are probably lodging a complaint as we speak."

He looked at her, and then the shared wall, then the headboard. He'd *shouted?*

She glanced at his face and set off again into gales of laughter. "Oh, I'm sorry, Ronan, it was so good. Earth-shatteringly good. And you … you *yelled.*"

"So you mentioned."

She curled up into his body. "Not so reserved then." She yawned. Her breathing evened out, deepened.

She twitched once, muttered, and was asleep. "You neither," he whispered.

He stared down at the woman in his arms. What the hell had just happened? And not just that insanely hot sex. He made it a point never to be around girlfriends—hell, anyone if he could help it—after a loss. But this woman, she'd accepted it. Him. The losing. And he'd let her. That was the part that confounded him. He didn't like anyone, not even the women he dated—especially not the women he dated—to see him brought down by a loss. Defeated, vulnerable, and angry. He'd thought it wasn't the kind of thing partners should be subjected to. Cass had blown right through that. And he wasn't quite sure how.

Chapter 7

Cass had the morning to herself in her opulent hotel room. She'd snuck out of Ronan's suite in the wee hours and slept until nearly nine. Starving and unwilling to bring herself to head down to one of the restaurants, she had ordered room service. That had been an eighty-dollar mistake. She'd planned to hit the spa for a massage, but that breakfast had sent her hotel budget out the window. Despite the trust fund, she was naturally conservative with money. Or had been until now. This trip and its excesses were a blip. Once she got home, she'd go back to living within her paycheck.

The day after a race, the Pantech-Windsor crew would be busy packing up the cars and shipping everything to the next destination, rather like packing up a small army of personnel and equipment. Ronan had explained the process—special cargo planes, specially designed crates for the cars, plus arrangements for the hundred or so people who were part of the team, including the two drivers. It could be a logistical nightmare in some countries with the mix of bureaucratic red tape, corruption, and fragile equipment.

Ronan called at eleven.

"How are you?" he asked.

"Good, you?"

"Better than I usually am after a loss. Thanks for … well, thanks."

"It was fun."

Understatement of the year.

"So," he cleared his throat, "you don't ride, do you?"

"Horses? Or do you mean camels? Neither if I can help it."

"No, motorcycles, or more specifically, dirt bikes."

"Oh. Yeah, of course."

"You've ridden dirt bikes?"

She laughed. "What haven't I ridden? Motorcycles, dirt bikes, ATVs, Jet Skis. All that stuff. I grew up in Gateway, Arizona, remember?"

"Don't know it."

"Desert."

"Ah. See? I know nothing about you. Small town?"

"Kinda," she replied. "I traveled the world as a tot with my mom and Anderson. Then she got sick of it and took me back to the States, back to her hometown."

"So you are a world traveler?"

She laughed. "I was. I think I was six when mom and I settled in Gateway."

"So you went to school there?"

"No, my hometown is tiny and the schools are pretty low ranked. Anderson convinced her to put me in private school outside Phoenix, but the commute just about killed my mom. So they sent me to boarding school from seventh grade on."

"Boarding school? Is that common in the States?"

"Not really. Rockmont was a small, private, expensive prep in New Hampshire. Not really my crowd—more your crowd. Then when I was in high school, my mom started dating Jim, and I started getting into trouble. Nothing major. Breaking curfew, drinking—the usual teen rebellion crap. Anyway, Mom married Jim, and the next thing I knew, they took me out of Rockmont and back to Gateway for my senior year."

"Transplanted in high school? That can't have been fun."

"It was beyond awful. I was a fish out of water and a total snob. And I hated living with Jim and my mom. Jim and I only reached a truce after he took me out flying. Once I got in the cockpit I was hooked."

"So you didn't go to university?"

"My mom didn't agree with the pilot career trajectory, so she insisted I do two years of college."

"That's funny. I was prep school turned driver—everyone I knew in high school are all barristers now, or doctors, and I'm the blue collar worker."

"Yes—transportation, like me," she said, laughing. "Only your pay grade is higher."

"Would you be up for motorbikes on the dunes?"

"God, yes. But are you allowed?"

"How do you mean?"

"I mean don't they have insurance on you?"

A pause. "Bollocks to that. No one dictates my leisure activities."

"Alrighty then."

Two hours later, Cass selected a helmet from the shelves while Ronan paid. She hadn't expected him to pay, but he was too quick whipping out that credit card to give her a chance.

He joined her at the back of the shop. She watched him approach, tucking his wallet into the back pocket of his jeans. He was so confident in his stride, the way he handled himself. She'd had that kind of confidence, once upon a time. Before she'd killed someone. She pushed those thoughts away.

"You okay?" he asked, frowning.

What was it with this guy? He was so tuned in to her. It made him a phenomenal lover, but it was a bit off-putting when she had things she didn't want to share.

"Would you let me get something one of these days?"

"Get something?"

"Pay."

"I expect I make more than you do—"

True, her pilot salary had never crept up into the six-figure mark, no matter how much overtime she worked. "Well, yeah, considering I'm unemployed now, but I have savings. I may not be in your league, but I'm far from destitute."

"You're on leave, yes?"

Until they fire me. "It doesn't sit well with me." She gestured to the man in front of the register at the front of the store.

"You know what I made last year," he said awkwardly. It was common knowledge. His salary was posted on the Internet. It wasn't the highest F1 paycheck at twenty million dollars, but it wasn't far off. Then there were the sponsorships. His longevity in the sport combined with his visits to the podium parlayed into an obscenely large paycheck.

"I'd just feel more comfortable paying sometimes."

His expression registered surprise. "I like to pay." He grinned. "Puts me in charge."

"In your dreams," she retorted.

She stared at the shelves of colorful Arai helmets. He selected his helmet—blue and black.

Boring.

"Really? Thank God you have sponsors who put you in vibrant attire—I can only imagine what you'd look like if left to your own devices." She pulled a yellow and green helmet with a lightning bolt off the shelf. "Try this brain bucket."

"Brain bucket? I like this one. You go pick your own."

"But this one's gorgeous. Take it." She extended her arm and gave it a shake.

He shook his head.

The light dawned. "Oh, it has to be blue, doesn't it?"

His eyes widened almost imperceptibly.

"Ronan, seriously? What is this fixation with that color?" She pressed her lips together to keep the grin at bay.

He shifted his feet, not meeting her eyes, and she burst out laughing. "You are so superstitious. I can't credit it."

"All drivers are."

"About everything? Is it lucky for me I have blue eyes? Would I be less appealing if they were hazel or brown?" she teased him. "Does the same apply to you? Your balls—"

He leaned down with a growl to capture her laughing mouth, pushing her back into the wall next to the shelving. Her arms curled around the thick, strong column of his neck, all traces of levity banished with the press of his body, she opened her mouth to the slick search of his tongue. Arousal coiled through her as she stretched into him, sucking his lower lip. Her hands fisted in his hair as she held his mouth to hers.

Laughter from the other end of the store recalled her circumstances, and she released his neck. Maneuvering her hands to the front of his shirt, she pressed him from her.

He groaned, adjusting his jeans.

She glanced down with a giggle. "What was I saying?"

A short laugh escaped him. "Yes, now I feel so much luckier."

• • •

An hour later he got off the bike, legs shaking, put down the stand, and yanked off his helmet, livid, as he stalked over. "What the hell do you think you're doing?"

She pushed up her visor, shifting her legs to balance the bike on the sand between them. "Having fun, same as you. What's your problem?"

"Going over the dune that way, in this crowd? Are you out of your mind altogether?"

"Don't be such an old woman. I know how to handle myself on the bike."

"You damn well don't. This place is notorious for wrecks with all the cars and ATVs and crap out there. You went over the edge of that dune blind."

Her chin went up. "It wasn't blind. And I knew I could land it. I knew where the other vehicles were. What's the big deal?"

"There are too many people here to chance something like that. Look. It's chaos!"

"Calm down. I'm fine. As you can see."

He raised a hand to his brow. That had been one hell of an idiotic move, and watching her vanish over the dune like that in heavy traffic had given him a bad moment. She was obviously experienced on the bike but with all these people in their appropriate and inappropriate vehicles racing up and down the dunes willy-nilly, cresting the dune like that was sheer stupidity. Was she …?

He moved closer. "Have you been drinking?"

Her face shuttered. "Of course not. What do you take me for? I would never drink and drive anything."

He peered at her, her face set in angry lines. Fine, let her be angry. "Let's go."

They had been having a good time—he'd never done anything like this with a woman. His mates, yeah. Dozens of times when he was younger. And he'd reveled in a strange sort of pride mixed with awe watching her ride her dirt bike up and down the dune, her lithe body balancing on the machine. That was, until she'd performed that stunt. Now she revved the engine, turning the bike so the rear tire spat sand all over him. He cursed, and his arm flew up to protect his eyes and mouth from flying sand. Still muttering to himself, he put his helmet back on. Not for the first time, he found himself wondering about the circumstances of her helicopter accident … and why he was afraid of those answers.

Ronan collected his deposit and went through the process of checking in the motorbikes, vaguely aware that Cass was at the counter to return their helmets. So she was giving him the silent treatment, was she? Well he was just as pissed as she. More so.

He held the door for her as she left the shop, then practically raced her to the car to open that door. She muttered her thanks, closing the door of the rented Mercedes with more force than necessary. He hid his smile walking around the rear of the vehicle. Slamming the door of a new Mercedes just didn't have the same effect it did in most cars. It closed with a gentle thwack, not a loud clang.

He climbed in and fitted the key into the ignition. "Are we going to talk about it?"

"Not if it means another reprimand," she retorted.

"You scared me," he admitted.

"I wasn't unsafe," she said. "I knew who was coming up the dune from my last run and how fast they were going."

"Well I didn't, and from my vantage it looked foolhardy."

"It wasn't."

"I don't want to argue about it, Cass, I already told you it gave me a bad moment."

"So? Apologize."

"Me?" She wanted him to apologize for caring about her safety?

"I've spent my life in a career dominated by men, Ronan. And plenty of them have wanted to look out for me, or treat me with their brand of misplaced paternalism. I don't look for it, don't appreciate it. In fact, I resent the hell out of it. I'm your equal out there on those bikes, Ronan."

"I never said you weren't." He sat back. "I see what you're saying. And I think you're half right—I wouldn't have said the same thing to one of my mates. I might have thought 'what an idiot, doing that here,' but you gave me a bad moment not because of some misplaced paternalism but because …"

This was the tricky part. Sod it. Who cared if he sounded like a smitten schoolboy? "I like you."

She sat silently, staring at him. Then she smiled and the lightness of it chased all traces of anger from her face. "I like you too, Ronan."

Chapter 8

A week later, Ronan was far from the desert sun of Abu Dhabi, staring at the clouds thickening above the British countryside. He eased open the door of his motor home, took a whiff of the mustiness and faux lemon air-freshener, and threw his luggage on the bed. Someone from the team would come later with the rest. He set up the coffeemaker and then headed out again to say hello to the Silverstone track.

A sheet of drizzle whipped his face, and he turned his cheek against it. "Ah, you'll stop when I need you to," he yelled into it. "The BBC said so." He flung his smooth stone across the gritty tarmac. Four bounces. Perfect. Gathering it up, he trekked back to the caravan. He stepped inside and rubbed his hands, switched on the heaters, poured a coffee into his lucky *Top Gear* mug, and dragged a chair to the window so he could survey the track—one of the oldest F1 circuits in the world.

He drank the hot coffee gratefully. The plan for today was to pay a visit to the team. Always good to see the guys in the factory who never made it to the regular races. Then the gym. Then—if all worked out—Cass. As the late Lou Reed would say, a perfect day.

He looked at her name on his phone's speed dial and calculated. She'd told him they would arrive at Heathrow at eleven and were staying at the Whittlebury Hotel adjacent to the circuit. They should be checked in by now, even if the traffic was horrendous. He pressed dial. "How're you doing?"

"Ronan? Oh, fine, fine. We just got here." Her voice was muffled like she was in a car, and slightly breathless, but it ignited a spark of excitement in his gut. "Took us nearly an hour to get from Towcester, but we found the hotel okay. Speaking of which, um, we nearly ran over Maddux at the entrance."

"Ran over Maddux?" Ronan laughed. "That's my job, Cass, but I appreciate the intent."

"No, it was terrible! Anderson's still outside apologizing to him. I don't know whether I should get out, too, now, or—"

"I'd let Anderson handle it. The guy would sue for millions if you as much as broke his toenail. His own bloody fault for standing in a driveway."

"So where are you?"

"In my caravan by the track."

"How is it? I'm picturing a mobile home with a single door and window and red-checkered curtains."

"Not far off," he laughed, fingering the functional horizontal blinds. "Why don't you come over and help me warm it up?"

A slight pause. "Um. Well, let me get checked in here and I'll come find you. Am I allowed near this trailer? How will I find it?"

"I'll send you the GPS coordinates. Connect to my wifi, password Lana1."

"Lana, huh?"

"My car."

"Ah." Another pause. "So is this place private, or are you overrun with engineers and crew?"

"Just me," he said.

"Does the door even lock?"

"Why? Are you planning on doing something naughty?"

"You tell me. I'm wearing something blue."

A smile spread across his face.

• • •

He left the motor home to search for her disguised in a Navy anorak and Wellington boots, with a baseball cap pulled low and brandishing a large umbrella—looking, he hoped, more like a regular F1 enthusiast than a horny driver. He could do without the press vultures chasing him and swooping down on her.

A large crowd had amassed along the fence in front of the McLaren and Ferrari garages. He could barely see a thing. How would he find her? He craned his neck to find the epicenter. Someone poked his side. He turned and found himself drowning in the familiar, captivating blue eyes of Cassidy Miller. His heart gave an extra whump. He grabbed her shoulders, fighting the urge to kiss her. "Mmm, Cass." He bent closer and murmured. "Let's get out of here before someone recognizes me."

She hooked her arm onto his, smiling up. "I'm all for that."

Settling his hand into the sculpted small of her back, he steered her away from the garages, tugging his cap farther down. "What the hell's that all about?" he said. "They're not showing off the cars now."

"Oh, I think that had something to do with Maddux handing out cans of Supernova through the fence. I couldn't get anywhere near close enough to see, but that's what someone told me."

He snorted. "Cheap PR trick. Wait 'til they actually taste it."

She looked back and grinned. "Let's hope he has enough cans for the whole crowd."

He sighed. "Keep moving."

"Where is it?" She gave him that look—the lustful one—and something tugged at his stomach and then lower down. His body throbbed to life.

"We're almost there."

"That one?" She pointed.

"No, Cass, that's a storeroom. I'm over here."

"Okay, little bigger than I expected. Is it all yours?"

"Look." He held up the keys. "If it's any reassurance, these here are the only keys, and they're mine and mine only. We *will* be alone."

• • •

He held the flimsy door of the motor home open for her. She took the two metal steps into the trailer.

"I put the heat on. It's often too effective for such a small space, so let me know if you get too hot." He smiled playfully. "I often strip down when I come in here."

Cass nodded, taking it all in. It was tiny—narrow aisles, a galley kitchen with recessed cabinets, and what looked to be a bedroom at the far end—but it was immaculate. She walked toward the kitchen, bending to search the fridge. Sodas, water, and energy drinks. Figured.

"Tempting view." He hadn't moved from the door.

"So this is where you stay?"

"I don't sleep here." He took two steps forward. "I use this place to—decompress."

She eyed him. "Is that a euphemism for something?"

He looked taken aback, then laughed. "No. Who do you think I am? James Hunt?"

Her brow wrinkled. "I know that name …"

"An F1 driver. One of the greats. But he had a habit of bedding thousands of women in the seventies. He was our sport's Wilt Chamberlain."

"So this is not where you bring your track bunnies? After your wins and all the milk drinking?"

He sighed. "Indianapolis 500."

She grinned. He was so easy to tease. "Oh, right. You guys do it up all classy, with champagne on the podium."

She peered down the hall. "Judging by the state of this place, I don't need to worry about the sheets."

He placed a box of condoms on the table opposite the kitchen.

Heat surged through her. What was it about Ronan? She tried to mask it, but being with him put her continually on edge.

Excited, expectant—anticipating. And he knew it, if his cocky grin was anything to go by. James Hunt, indeed. Well, all these drivers had an excess of everything—money, women, things. And it wasn't like she entertained any hopes for a future for them—she and Ronan lived on opposite sides of the planet. Yet the thought of him with someone else sent a bolt of jealousy through her, cramping her stomach. She would not have that conversation. This thing, this whatever it was, was a distraction, nothing more, no matter how much she liked him.

His hand lifted her chin. "Penny for your thoughts?"

"My thoughts are lustful," she admitted, meeting his intense hazel gaze.

His lids drooped, and he got that sleepy look he had whenever he was aroused. Excitement throbbed through her. "Now that's an interesting turn in the conversation." He edged closer, then bent, his lips covering hers, his tongue teasing her lips then slipping inside without hesitation.

Lifting her effortlessly, he set her on the little Formica kitchen counter. She wiggled until she managed to hitch up her skirt.

"And here I was worried you were going to keep prattling on about the Indianapolis 500." He stepped between her legs, yanking her toward him. They were separated only by the thin cotton of her panties and his well-worn jeans. Heat emanated from him. She drew back long enough to lift her cotton shirt over her head and toss it away. Her hands moved over his shirt, then under the fabric to the smooth, hard flesh of his stomach.

He took a gasping breath, his abdominal muscles twitching as she ran the palm of her hand down to the waistband of his pants, unsnapping and unzipping, delving into the elastic band, then under to his throbbing cock. He thrust into her greedy palm with a groan. She wrapped a hand around his cock and his face flushed with desire.

Her lips curved, and she reached up, wrapping one hand around the back of his neck, pulling him down to her impatient mouth.

He lifted her bottom with one hand, sliding and tugging with the other until he'd liberated her from her panties. She glanced down where they'd landed on the linoleum floor between his legs.

He tugged her bottom to the edge of the counter, the cold Formica a stark contrast to his heat. Spreading her legs wider, he reached down and stroked, teasing her, finding her clit. Her teeth tugged on her bottom lip to stifle a groan. She closed her eyes and threw her head back—banging it on the cabinet door.

"Ow."

He made a contrite sound, and one hand came around the back of her head to rub the injured spot. His other hand still stroked circles slowly, so slowly, until he pushed two fingers into her. Involuntarily, her body clamped down on them, and she lifted her hips. His fingers thrust, too gently, while his thumb rubbed and pressed on her. She was panting now, fighting back her orgasm. He knew her body so well.

She reached up for a kiss, her tongue tangling with his, his fingers mimicking the thrust of his tongue. Oh God. She was desperate to come.

• • •

Ronan shoved his pants and underwear down. His cock sprang free; there was no way they were going to make it the six feet to the bedroom. He couldn't wait. Easing her legs farther apart, he fumbled for the condom box with shaking hands.

Cass, panting, took the disc from him, tore the wrapper, and stroked it on, pausing to press and squeeze until he knocked her hands away and positioned her for his entry.

Her hands came back to torment him. This time he manacled her hands in his and pressed them above her head, against the cabinet. Her hair covered much of her face, a face flushed with lust.

One eye peeked out from the masses of chestnut hair. "Ronan, please. Now, already," she said.

He guided the head of his cock into her entrance. Her body resisted a bit, so he held the base, working himself into her one exquisite inch at a time. She was making a low keening sound. She was close. "Yes" he murmured, fascinated by her naked desire.

He stroked her, circling, until she bucked into his hand, crying out his name, her inner muscles clenching. He gritted his teeth, holding himself back, waiting until she was spent, then he drove into her, pushing in to the hilt, over and over until he came with a loud shout.

•••

She sat up in the bed. He watched her pull the sheets up around her breasts protectively, staring into space. She'd whimpered in her sleep and then jerked once; that was it. No panicked murmuring.

"Hey there, gorgeous," he said.

For a moment she looked confused. "I slept, didn't I?" It sounded self-accusatory.

He whipped back the covers and sat up, trailing his fingers down her shoulder, and planted a kiss. "Not for long. A power nap I'd call it."

"Did I say anything?"

Was this about the nightmares? She hadn't stayed overnight in his room since … ever. He frowned. "No, why? Are you still dreaming, about the accident? That first night you did—I think you did at any rate. You were talking about flying in your sleep."

She hugged the sheet to herself. "Yes," she said, dully, not meeting his eyes. "I have nightmares."

He stroked her back but she flinched, so he removed his hand. "You never stay the night. Is that why?"

Now she did meet his gaze, her expression shuttered. "Of course not. It's because this is," she waved a hand dismissively, "it's … casual."

Something tightened up in his stomach at her words. "So?"

"So, I go back to my room. I don't want to be caught sneaking out of yours. It may not be great for Anderson if this gets around."

He climbed out of the bed and stepped into his boxer briefs, doing his best to shove aside whatever was pushing his panic button at her casual treatment of their connection. How could she be so nonchalant? "Want coffee? Soda?"

"Got anything stronger?" Her gaze wandered over the kitchen area.

"No. Sorry, I'm not exactly well prepared for guests."

"Coffee's fine," she said.

"Good." He retrieved his mug from the window ledge and got a new one for her. Just as he went to grab the coffee jug, the phone buzzed.

"Hey, Benny, what's up?" he said, unable to keep the irritation from his tone.

"Check out the *Herald* evening edition sports section. They've news on your father."

"My—?" Ronan let the phone fall on the bed, pulled out his laptop, and began typing furiously. "Shit," he breathed. The article prattled on about him and his father. The scandal. The rumors. It was all there again. Stuff that had been put to rest long ago. Now, news of his father's impending release was churning it up all over again. Warning bells started clanging in his ears.

Fucking Harry.

The sole reason he hated coming to race in the U.K. People had long memories here for this stuff. The British press never let it lie. He grasped the phone again. "Sorry, Benny, had to check for myself. Thanks for the heads up. Call you later."

He set the phone down. "What shitty timing," he said.

"Something wrong?" Cass emerged from the bedroom, her eyes bright with concern.

He sat down blindly, his mind overcrowded with memories and anger. He turned the laptop screen so she could view the story.

She read aloud from the article on the screen, "Harry Hawes, convicted fraudster and father of F1 driver, Ronan Hawes, is due for release from Springhill Prison on 24 November. Hawes was the confirmed instigator of a Ponzi scheme in London that caused a loss of 120 million pounds, robbing some sixty couples of their retirement savings. His release coincides with this year's final F1 race in Germany."

"He's getting out," Ronan said unnecessarily.

Cass looked from him to the computer screen. "I'm sorry seems like the wrong thing to say about a member of family getting out of prison."

"Trust me, it isn't."

She wrapped an arm around his waist and he held her against him, staring at his father's mug shot, the release date, 24 November burning into his retinas. He couldn't let it cloud his thoughts. There was a race to win tomorrow. On home soil.

Chapter 9

"Ronan, I'm still out of breath," squawked a reporter. "You're in flying form. Second last year, top podium step this year. Tell us!" The throngs of newscasters pressed up against the stage. Ronan's ears still rang from the blare of the circuit and the ecstatic roars of the crowd as he'd stepped out of the car. Nothing could replace the taste of victory. He'd floated all the way over to the press conference tent on a testosterone high.

He wiped his brow, grinning into the cameras. "Honestly, I don't know. First of all, it's phenomenal to race in front of this crowd, so thanks to the fans. It's unbelievable. One of the best races all season. The car was fantastic. It was a bit tight at the start; Supernova had a good lead and I didn't know whether I'd be able to pull it off." Ronan shook his head to dispel the memory of sheer terror when he had been two cars behind Maddux. "I just tried to focus on my driving. We had incredible pace again in the car, and I managed to control the gaps … to come here and win the race is incredible. I don't know what to say."

"Maybe that your luck has come at last?"

Ronan turned to the pretty female reporter, keeping his grin intact. "Well, I'd like to think so. I believe in luck," he said. "And it comes from being in the right place at the right time and with the right people—my team, my sponsors, and of course, a little something extra this season." That set the reporters into a flurry of excitement as hands shot up to ask the next question. Just as expected.

"Is it a woman? Who is she?"

"Tell us," yelled another.

"Are you back with Vivienne McCloud?"

He allowed the room to return to relative calm as they hung on his next answer.

"Will she be in Texas with you?"

"Um …" Ronan's eyes roamed the crowd of invitation-only reporters as if looking out for someone. The wall clock blinked 17:15 P.M. He'd made it. Now he could wrap this baby up before they got a chance to ask him about—

"Ronan, your father, Harry Hawes—"

Ronan bolted forward and clicked off the microphone. He waved in dismissal to the frenzied reporters and gave his PR agent sitting on his left a jovial slap on the shoulder. "Time's up, Bill. What do you say we go stretch our legs and grab a drink?" With a final wave, he stood and started talking to the engineering team off to the side.

Feigning total obliviousness to the reporters, Ronan clearly heard the reporter's insistent voice. "It's been speculated that his release from prison will be just before the qualifiers for Hockenheim. What do you think about this?" He tried not to think about Harry, now or ever. Why couldn't the world just forget about the stupid old fool? What did he have to do to wipe the mud off the Hawes name for once and for all? Would becoming F1 world champion put those rumors that he somehow benefited from his father's crimes to rest? Well, it was all he had to offer.

He made it over to the VIP tent without a single reporter accosting him, which was a feat almost as impressive as his win today. He couldn't wait to see Cass.

"Ronan!" She stood before him, alone and glorious in a light gray, figure-hugging dress with a blue, swirly shawl that wafted across her collarbone. He pulled her in tight. "Mmm."

She pushed back with a ferocity that stunned him. "How could you do that?"

"Do what?"

Her eyes blazed an angry, glinting blue. "Mention me!"

He stepped back. She was seething, ready to combust. "Mention you? I—I didn't." Had he? He could scarcely remember what had been asked or answered in that PR session. All he could remember was the heat on him when Harry popped up in the conversation.

"You gave them a broad enough hint!"

"What?"

"Bit of extra luck? What the fuck, Ronan. What's next? Tossing my panties out into the audience?"

"Hey, I—" he said.

Her expression remained furious. He reached for her free arm, but she withdrew it.

"Cass?"

"And when they come after me?" Her eyes were haunted. "What then? What are you going to say when word of my accident gets out? What am I going to say? And Anderson?"

"I'm sorry, Cass. I think they might focus on your being a pilot, not the accident." He sighed. "It comes with the territory. As far as Anderson goes? He's not my sponsor; I don't think there's a conflict there." He stepped back and folded his arms, all the warmth seeping from his body. "The more you win, the worse it gets."

She held her hands to the sides of her head. "Oh God."

He considered the options and shrugged. "I don't know what to say, Cass. I've never had this discussion before. This being in the public eye thing is my least favorite part of racing. The better I do, the more they pry and the more crap they put out there," he said. "They'll make up any old shite if they have to, to sell papers, sell tickets. I ignore it as much as I can. And F1 sees nearly all publicity as good for the sport. You're the first person I've been with who's had any problem with it."

"I can't believe that."

He shrugged. "It's true."

"The women you've dated haven't had a problem being put under the microscope?"

"Never."

"Why not?"

He shrugged. "You'd have to ask them. Some of them were used to it. A couple were well known in their own right. But you with your—"

She stiffened.

"I'm not used to someone who sees the press, the publicity, as such a drawback," he amended hastily.

She twisted her hands together. "Huge drawback. Huge."

"Well, the women I've dated have tended to see it more as a benefit."

"I want to be very clear about this. I don't. You don't mention me. You don't say my name. You don't even *allude* to me."

He gave a laugh that came out more like a groan. Part of the reality of being Ronan Hawes the last few years was that the women he dated wanted to date an F1 driver. A winner. With all the perks that came with it. Like most of the guys he raced with, he wasn't the most sociable person on the planet. In fact, half of the drivers were downright introverted. He'd learned to work with the press, and could talk shop with his fans, but connecting with strangers wasn't his favorite pastime. The women he dated, particularly Viv, were great with strangers, the press, the cameras, all of it. Most had been accustomed to public scrutiny in their own careers as models, actresses—even the barrister he'd dated had been a pro with the media. Hell, Viv had been a journalist and then a television presenter.

But it was both a blessing and a curse. His lovers' comfort and appreciation of the "life" did lead him to question their motivations on occasion. Particularly Viv's. Their relationship had helped her career. There was no denying that, and he didn't begrudge it. She saw them as a power couple; there was no denying that either.

But the real reason he'd never been able to commit to her was that he had never been sure if it was Ronan Hawes F1 driver she'd loved, or Ronan Hawes from Tunbridge Wells. They'd never fought, never argued, and although there had been chemistry in bed, there'd been no passion out of it.

The women he'd been involved with appreciated things in his life that he only tolerated. Vivienne reveled in it. Clearly Cass was nothing like Viv. Cass was more like him: eschewing crowds and all the socializing with strangers, but hotheaded too. And despite her father's affluence, she wasn't part of this world. Even after ten years, navigating it could still be a challenge for him. He opened his mouth to explain some of this, but when the words came out they sounded like, "I just need to focus on my driving and win."

She looked him up and down as if he were an exhibit at Madame Tussauds. She backed up a step.

"Oh no you don't." He reached out and grabbed her gently. "Don't walk off on me. I'm sorry it's out there. We'll do what we can to mitigate speculation about you. Want me to say that you're my cousin thrice removed?"

"It's not funny, Ronan."

He nodded, letting go.

She turned on her heel.

Heading for the bar no doubt.

He'd withdrawn from Viv because there hadn't been enough passion in the relationship. Was there such a thing as too much? He could understand where Cass was coming from, and she'd already told him she wanted to keep their relationship out of the spotlight. She was right, of course. He had thrown her under the bus as she'd said, hoping to divert attention from Harry's release.

She practically ran into someone in her haste to get away. Great, just what this evening needed yet: Maddux. Of course. The sleazy-eyed idiot was putting on his best schmoozing pose, head cocked, grin as wide as a Cheshire cat, arm movements expansive.

Sickening. Maddux swiped the empty glass off Cass and was evidently going to fetch her another drink. How gallant. No, he was hesitating ... leaning in toward her, whispering something.

Ronan took eight strides over to them.

She stared at Maddux, ignoring Ronan at her side. "No thanks, Maddux. Now run along and get the bourbon for me, would you?"

Maddux's green eyes slid from him to her and back again, obviously disinclined to leave them alone again.

"May I suggest we get the hell out of here before they snap a few photos of this little *ménage a trois,*" Ronan said. taking her arm and deftly avoiding a particularly gossipy Formula One blogger approaching. "And so I can apologize properly?"

She followed him to the exit door.

"Well?" She stared at him, arms crossed.

"You're right. I'm sorry."

"I thought you understood. About the press thing, I ..."

"I do," he said, "but all I could think of was putting something out there that would take them off the scent of Harry. Ill-advised self-preservation. I didn't think," he admitted. "I'm sorry. Let me make it up to you. Tell me you don't need to pack to leave early tomorrow or anything."

"I'm here for two days. Anderson has business engagements near the circuit and asked me to hang around, too. So I'm here 'til at least Tuesday."

"I'd like to take you away from all this. God knows I'd like to get away from it, too. And, I know a great place—"

"Reporter-free?"

"Yes. It's called Danesfield House. And you'd love it there. Just an overnighter, but it's this wonderful hotel out in the country—a mansion, really—with massive grounds, quiet, with views of the Thames and—"

"Okay."

He looked down at her. Some of the familiar warmth had returned to her face. "Aren't you going to ask about the spa treatment facilities, the mode of transport to get there, the time needed, and the quality of the food?"

She cocked her head. "Ronan, we just had sex in a trailer on a gravelly old F1 circuit. It can hardly go downhill from there."

He wrapped an arm around her, leaning heavily. "Oh we are high maintenance today."

She bore his weight, with a smile. "I'm sure you can handle whatever I throw at you."

"All right, I'll pick you up from your hotel at eight and we'll leave all this nonsense behind."

...

Cass watched the lush English countryside in the summer twilight whizzing past the tinted windows of the taxi. They'd voted to get a driver as neither had felt inclined to get behind a wheel this evening. Her mind was still reeling from the fight they'd had, Ronan's near slip up, and his genuine attempt to get things back to a calmer level between them. He was good at that. And he always made the effort, which was more than she could say for any other guy she'd dated. Once she'd reassured herself that the chauffeur—a tough-looking, wizened lady in her sixties—wasn't some reporter or some pervert keen on following their every move, she leaned into Ronan's shoulder, sighing. "This is nice. We've never actually gone somewhere together. We just meet up at races."

"Yes." His arm snuggled behind her lower back. "It's about time we did something. I was thinking." He turned to her. "What about a mini holiday?"

Cass tripped her fingers up his pants leg.

He groaned and trapped her hand.

The driver watched them gravely for a few seconds in the rearview mirror before impassively flicking her attention back to the front view.

Where could they go, given that she didn't want to fly? What about ...

"Venice!" she said.

"Venice? Good choice."

"I've never been to Italy."

"That's almost criminal. But I won't harp on about it. My travel in the States has been limited. Venezia, Italia, here we come."

Wow, he was actually serious about this. "When?"

"That one's easy. I have a week off after three weeks in Asia. So, four weeks from now?"

"Sounds good."

The car turned off the highway, and Cass saw a sign for the hotel. Minutes later they pulled onto a small hedgerow-lined drive.

"Lunch?" he asked as the bell-hop took their luggage.

"I'm starving," she admitted.

Ronan was right about the massive grounds. Danesfield House in Buckinghamshire sat perched on a hilltop with expansive views toward Chiltern Hills with its woods and gentle waterfalls. He'd stayed there a few times, and assured her that the facilities and cuisine were top notch. As if she cared.

Both Ronan and Anderson took their stays at four-star hotels and meals at Michelin-rated restaurants for granted. She'd lived half her life as a pilot in a doublewide trailer at an airport, grabbing a bite at the local diner. Yet while neither man was remotely stuck-up or snobbish, they were comfortable living in the lap of luxury in a way she wasn't, and would never be. "Are we anywhere close to where you grew up?"

A flicker of distaste crossed his expression. "I'm from Tunbridge Wells, south of London, a good eighty miles from here." He leaned back heavily in his chair glancing around. She stared at him, but he wouldn't look at her.

"Blue-collar? Upper-crusty? I'm not familiar with the area, and I'm curious about your background."

"Upper-middle, on the cusp of upper-crusty, as you'd say. Until it all fell apart."

She propped her chin into her hands. "Do you ever go back?"

"No." Ronan swiped a hand through his hair. "After everything went down with my father, my mother moved to New York and remarried. I've two half-siblings over there I've met a couple times in London."

"Not close then?"

"She's got her own life. Quite happy with her new man and two daughters."

"I see."

"I do call her on her birthday but that's about the extent of it."

"I get it. Anderson and I were never estranged, but we've only become close since my visit here. How long will you be in England?"

"I've got 'til Wednesday. Have to see the engineers back at the garages in Silverstone and start preparing for Asia. You know, already setting the clock forward and all that."

He filled her in on race preparations, the constant adjustments to the vehicles, the stringent test runs, the physical fitness routines. His comments were eye opening to someone like her who had once thought F1 drivers lived a charmed life. They didn't. A prisoner had more liberties.

"Ronan to Cass. Come in, Cass."

"Oh!" She put down her glass and smiled. "Sorry."

"I said, do you want another drink or will we, um, check out the room furnishings?"

"The furnishings," she smiled, licking the remnants of the drink from her lips. "Yes to checking out the room. You never know. The standards may have slipped since the last time you stayed here."

"Then we need a thorough test," he said, guiding her along.

Fifteen minutes later she sat on the edge of the bed while he stood over her, watching, his chest heaving as she tore open the packet and pulled out the rubber disc. She took him in her hand, and he grunted. She cupped his balls, which were already taut against his body, and put her mouth on him.

He backed up a step as a shudder ripped through him and said hoarsely, "Whoa. I can't … don't do that, I'm barely hanging on just looking at you."

She met his intense, hazel gaze, rolled the condom on, and he pushed her back on the bed, into the soft, cold, white sheets. She shivered, though whether from nerves, excitement, or the chill in the room, she couldn't have said. "You feel so good," she murmured, her hands stroking his body shoulder to thigh, lingering to yank his hips hard against her. There was so much of him, and he radiated heat.

He pressed his mouth to her, holding his body above her with his hands on the bed. She arched and moaned beneath him, wanting the press of his flesh against hers. He rolled off to the side and stroked one shaking hand down the front of her body. He stopped to cup one breast and toy with her nipple, rolling it between his fingers, his eyes half shut with arousal.

She bit her lip, holding back a moan.

Never breaking eye contact, he ran the wide palm of his hand down over her stomach as her muscles there twitched and fluttered. He rubbed her, sliding one finger into her; her body clenched around it, and he drew in a sharp breath at her gasp. Another finger joined the first as his thumb circled her.

"I know you want to take it slow," she gasped out, "but … next time. I want you inside me now … please."

She stared up into his face, memorizing every line, his skin stretched taut with pleasure, his cheeks flushed.

Her body throbbed against his hand as his fingers continued to pulse into her body and he stroked her clit. She gripped his wrist and wrested it away. She was on the verge, and she'd be damned if she came without him.

Silently, Ronan spread her legs and entered her slowly, inch by inch, until she was scouring his back with her nails, sobbing in her urgency to have him inside.

He stared down at her, giving her time to adjust, but her orgasm was upon her. Before he'd even entered her fully, she closed her eyes, arching up to him as she came apart with a garbled cry.

His eyes were wild, and they never left hers as he pumped into her, over and over until at last he came with a guttural groan. He rolled his heavy, heaving body off her, settled her into the crook where his arm met his chest, and she faded out with the vision of his hazel eyes softening as he gazed at her.

•••

She leaned on the counter in the vanity and laid her forehead on the cold mirror—anything to avoid that face in the reflection— hating her bloodshot eyes with their dark rings. She'd never been one to wear much makeup, but these days she needed to buy stock in concealer. There was no disguising the haunted depths of her eyes, but she could at least make an attempt to hide the dark circles. When had she last slept through the night? The alcohol numbed her but made the nights restless and nightmare-ridden. Ronan had shaken her awake twice last night, hauling her into his big, warm body for comfort after her subconscious had taken her back to that night in the desert. She'd lain in his arms until he'd fallen back asleep, then had disentangled herself and crept from the bed.

She pressed her hands on the vanity as her heart rate accelerated.

Pulling up the tap lever for the tap, she filled the hotel glass. Took one sip, then another. Then her hand was shaking too badly to hold the glass and she put it down on the counter.

Oh God. Not here.

She cast a desperate glance at the door. It's 7:00 A.M. He'd be waking any minute to head to the gym.

"Cass?" His sleepy voice came from the door.

Calm down. Just calm down.

The shaking intensified, her heart thudded against her sternum. She searched the mirror, barely recognizing the flushed, terrified woman reflected at her.

She backed up two steps, slid down the wall to the floor, panting, and wrapped her arms around her knees.

Oh God, oh God.

Her brain was telling her she wasn't dying, but her body was sending another message entirely.

"Cass? Need to use the loo." Ronan rapped lightly.

"Just a … just …" She clenched her chattering teeth, her body drenched in cold sweat.

"Cass?" He sounded concerned now.

"D-d-d-don't …" she whispered.

How long had she been in here freaking out? Was it getting better or worse?

The door opened, Ronan stuck his head in, holding a hand in front of his eyes, probably worried about what he might see. "You, uh …"

"Here," she managed.

He looked down. "Cassidy, what the hell?"

"Panic."

He crouched down, gathered her up, and took her to the bedroom, where he sat with her in his lap on the edge of the bed.

She hung on to him, cheeks wet, the shaking finally diminishing, though her heart was still thundering.

Ronan stroked a hand down her back—long, comforting strokes, calming her.

He held her long after her heart rate went back to normal. Long after she needed him.

He started to speak but she covered his lips with a trembling finger.

Easing her out of his arms, he laid her in the bed, covering her with the sheets and comforter.

He left, and it was all she could do not to call him back. She heard the toilet flush, the water run, then shut off. The bed sagged as he climbed back in, pulling her into his body, holding her tightly, almost too tightly.

"Jesus, Cass, that was scary," he whispered into her hair. "Can we talk about it? Do you need a doctor or—"

"No doctor. Later, please? I just need sleep," she begged.

The heat radiating from his body, the comforting thud of his heart lulled her to sleep.

Chapter 10

"It's not just China," Ronan said softly, taking her hand in his, helping her into the private car that would take them to Silverstone. "It's Japan and Malaysia, too. Actually, Japan's first."

Cass squirmed in the seat. After a late night, planning a jet-setting schedule was headache inducing. Or was that a remnant of her panic attack this morning?

"It'll be a full month," she said.

"Right, but then Venice."

"Then Venice."

They'd had to leave the hotel by noon as Ronan was on a tight schedule. He was going to drop her off at Anderson's hotel in Silverstone and drive on to the garages where his engineering team was headquartered.

"I don't think I can face the travel to Asia right now." She studied his reaction in profile. All she could see was a slight denting in his cheek muscle and two rapid blinks. He turned to her. "That's okay. It's a grueling schedule." He grinned. "I'm tempted to skip it, too, and, you know, do some extracurricular stuff."

She cleared her throat. "Any of those tracks lucky for you then?"

"They'd be luckier if you were there."

"Be serious. Besides, you still have the panties, yes?"

"Of course. And I am serious."

"I'd like to be there," she said, "it's just … it's just the flight, you know? The flying is … hard. I have to get very drunk," she admitted. "That's how I managed to get over here. Poor Anderson. And then the state I was in going from Brussels to the UAE, I … I'm probably on some kind of watch list."

"I didn't realize. At least, not until this morning. Is that what happens if you fly?"

She nodded, staring out the window.

"Do you want to talk about it?"

"No." He'd seen more than enough this morning. Rehashing it wouldn't help him, or her.

"How many of those have you had?"

She turned back to him. His expression was concerned as the driver turned onto the highway.

"I don't want to—"

"Talk about it. Yeah. I know. Tough. We're talking about it. Is this because of the accident?"

"Yes."

"How many?"

She remained mute.

"Is it expected after a … trauma?"

She shrugged. "I assume. I was told I might have nightmares. Grief. You know."

"I'm sorry, but I don't know. I've never had that kind of experience."

"I just want to forget it."

"Are you sure? Isn't there someone you should be talking to? Or—"

Her fists clenched. Why did they all think a shrink was the magic bullet? And why did everyone from Anderson to her mother to Ronan couch it in the same terms: "someone you should talk to," which implied "not me, I don't know what to say" and "I don't want to know." The truth was they *didn't* want to know. Didn't even ask. Which was just as well because none of them could handle knowing what had gone down in the desert that night. How responsible she really was for the death of another person. And knowing that made her relationships feel like a lie. "I did talk to a crisis management team when it happened. We're required to. Then I had the meetings with the investigative teams from my company, the Federal Aviation Authority, everyone."

"Then tell me about the job."

"The job?"

"Yeah. You know enough about mine. I'd like to hear about yours."

"Think of me as an ambulance driver in the sky."

He laughed. "Think of me as a test car driver. Try again, Cass."

She exhaled a long breath. "I work in a pretty remote area in Arizona. My helicopter is, was, stationed at a small airport. About half of the calls we get are inter-hospital transport—small hospital to more specialized one. The rest are scene calls—"

"Accidents?"

"Yes—motor vehicle accidents, snakebites in the back country, stuff like that."

"Wow. So you land where exactly?"

"Hospitals or on the scene. If it's a scene call, law enforcement and the fire department usually get to the scene first and set up a landing zone away from power lines and trees and stuff."

"During the day?"

"Day, night, whenever."

"Wait. You land at these places at night?"

"Well, yeah, Ronan, there are accidents everywhere, night and day. So to get as close to the scene as we can, we land on highways, in elementary school parking lots, wherever we can find a safe spot."

"And you think *my* job is dangerous?"

"We wear night vision goggles."

"Cool."

"Way cool."

"You love it," he said, his tone registering surprise. "It's not just a job."

"Loved it," she corrected. She turned back to stare out the window, gloom settling over the car. "It was never just a job."

There was a long pause until Ronan said, "What will you do in London? I can give you a whole list of activities, you know."

"Like what? I'm not going to stand outside Buckingham Palace or watch *Phantom of the* goddamn *Opera*, or go to a wax museum."

"You'll see. There's a lot to do. And I'm going to Skype you for a full report of course." He caught her eye. "Every day."

She smiled. "Oh goody."

•••

"I'm not going to China," Cass announced an hour later, watching her father take the last swallow of his coffee. The hotel restaurant was deserted. Her mind and body were horribly sober. They'd be leaving for London within the next half hour.

Her father set down the porcelain cup. "I figured. I'll be gone three weeks though. You can stay in my London flat. That way you can walk or Tube anywhere you need to go. Or would you rather go home?"

"I'm not ready to go home."

"Well, you know where the race is after Asia, don't you?"

"Texas."

"Will you come with me to the Texas race?"

"Why not?" Her reply was breezy, but her blood ran cold. Texas was only a few hundred miles from Arizona. She'd done her EMS flight training there. She could drive home from Texas. It seemed Anderson was ready to send her back. And who could blame him? There was plenty of speculation already about her and Ronan. The F1 sponsor community was a small one. It had to be more awkward for Anderson than he was letting on.

"It'll be Thanksgiving a few days after the Circuit of The Americas race. Why don't you join Mom, Jim, and me for an early celebration?" If she was going to face her mother and stepfather, she could use Anderson's moral support. Jim hadn't let up. She had six unopened emails in her box. More nagging about finding a flying job before the investigation was complete, no doubt.

"Cass," he leaned forward, "is that what you want?" He took her hand and gave it a squeeze. "I'd be happy to go. I'll email your mother and see if it's acceptable to her."

Cass stared at him. "You'd be willing to do that, with Jim there?"

Anderson signaled the waiter for the check with a raised hand. "I'll stay at a hotel, of course, but sure. You know there's no animosity between your mother and me."

He signed his name on the slip and rose, obviously delighted with himself. "Sounds like a terrific plan."

"And you and Jim?"

"Don't worry, Cassidy." He extended a hand to help her up. "I've no quarrel with the man who helped raised you and helped you find your passion in life. He did a damned fine job."

She squelched the impulse to hurl herself into Anderson's arms.

• • •

Three weeks—nearly a whole month in London. A normal person would grab a friend to chatter and mindlessly shop with. But as girlfriends were thin on the ground, even back home, she was going to have to switch into waiting mode gracefully. Funny, just a month ago this solitude was exactly what she'd yearned for, what she'd followed Anderson to Europe for. Now it yawned before her like a prison sentence.

Ronan saying he'd Skype was all very well, but it didn't change the fact that she'd gone to bed alone the past five nights as he travelled to Japan and adjusted to the time zone. His one Skype call had been very late at night for him, and he'd needed to get to bed. She sat on the vast bed afterward, raiding her father's bar guiltily until getting slightly drunk. In fact, that had been the pattern since he'd left. She hadn't even had the wherewithal to go out to a liquor store and buy a decent bottle of bourbon.

She also, surprisingly, missed Anderson. Not just for the company itself and the sense of security, but also the quality of his company—his dry wit, his ever-present sense of compassion toward her. Of course, Anderson could be a bit much at times, too, but his departure left a gaping hole. She was back to being herself, left to her own devices. It was enough—almost—to make her want to get the first plane out to Nagoya.

Jim would be the first to tell her she was moping and feeling sorry for herself. Cass sighed and flipped open her phone to check the time—midnight. Maybe Ronan was available to chat after his morning workout session. She had to talk to him before the race in Suzuka tomorrow. Not that she was getting superstitious or anything, but she felt … uneasy at the thought of him racing without having at least talked to her first about the track, the dangers, the good parts, the strategy, what time he hoped for.

"Heyup." And there he was, grinning in to the screen, his sexy, half-naked body revealed as he toweled off his hair, then pulled on a baby blue Japanese kimono-type bathrobe that somehow managed to make her pulse leap. She must be desperate if the sight of a man in a kimono sent her heart racing.

"You'd love this place." He gestured to a delicate arrangement of pink orchids on the white table behind him. "Everything's so minimalistic, so serene." He smiled into the camera. "How's life back in the Old Smoke?"

Cass didn't survey the room with her phone in case he'd see the empty highball glasses on the TV table. She should've cleared it up. "I'm fine. Everything's … fine."

"Did you do anything yesterday?"

"Yesterday?" She shrugged. "Not much. It was raining."

He laughed. "If you let a spot of drizzle bother you, you won't get anywhere in London. There's a Japanese garden in Holland Park. I was just thinking of that today."

"Maybe another time," she said.

"Or take a train toward Lewisham, get out at Island Gardens, and go through the pedestrian tunnel under the Thames. Or get off at Greenwich and go to the maritime museum."

"I might try something indoors. You know, warm. It's chilly for October."

"Warm ..." Ronan rubbed his chin. "The Freud Museum? Charles Dickens Museum? The Royal Arcade on Old Bond Street."

"OK, you can stop there." She laughed, scribbling the names down, more as an act of compliance than anything. She wasn't in the mood for culture, for literature, for high-end shopping, for anything. Still, she might as well go to one of these just to be able to talk about it with him.

"So what have you been doing?" he asked, pulling on a crisp, white shirt.

"Oh ... this and that, you know."

Ronan lowered his eyebrows. "Not really, no."

"I went to Hyde Park." She'd seen it from a taxi. Close enough.

"Yes, always worth a look."

"Ready for tomorrow?" she said brightly.

"Yeah. It's a nice circuit. I like it anyway. The car's in top form." He squeezed his eyes shut and reopened them. "Just have to adapt to the time zone. Still feels like midnight somehow."

She did the math. "Which means you'll be driving early morning British time?"

"Yeah."

"Not your best time."

"Yours either."

They laughed in unison. "We know each other's weakness already," he said, clipping on his watch. He glanced at the clock face and frowned. "Oh damn, gotta finish dressing and go. Meeting at nine sharp with the head of engineering. But I … are you …?"

"Spit it out, Ronan."

"Are you okay? I worry about you there by yourself."

Warmth stole through her. "I'm fine," she replied.

"No panic?"

"None."

"Is that why you're not getting out? Are you afraid of the Tube or something?"

Her lips twisted. "No. Of course not. I'm just lazy, not afraid." But how true was that? Was that why she'd been holed up here in her dad's flat, bored out of her mind? It was easier to evade his questions hiding behind a screen like this. The thought of having a panic attack in public was terrifying.

• • •

The next morning she walked toward Bond Street. Of all the options, the arcade Ronan mentioned seemed the easiest. And goddamn it, she was tired of being so afraid—a prisoner in Anderson's luxurious condo. Bond Street was the "poshest" place to shop and sat on the highest-valued real estate in the country, according to one website. But it was situated close to Anderson's apartment. She planned on window-shopping; maybe she'd buy a book or travel guide.

Along the way, her eyes gravitated toward a red and white shirt in a dusty shop window across the street. It reminded her of something. So did the caps sitting below it. It was his Formula One colors, the exact same. This was an F1 fan shop. Without bothering to think, she made her way to the crosswalk. Here was something worth buying.

A bell jangled as she entered the dark shop's interior. A mid-sixties guy was folding T-shirts in front of the counter. He nodded to her with none of the loud pleasantries she'd have received in the States. But she preferred it this way. She fingered the shirt emblazoned with Ronan's name. His teammate Mitchell had a Pantech shirt, too. And drivers for the other teams like Trent, and Smith. A little cap with "Hawes" on the front called to her, so she tried it on in the mirror. By now the elderly shopkeeper was eyeing her. She guessed not many women entered his den of racing enthusiasm.

She removed the hat and tiptoed over to some brightly colored silk items on the table. "Hmm, what are these?" she mused aloud.

"They're neckties, ma'am. Great present for a man in your life what likes Formula One and Ronan Hawes in particular."

"Oh, the man in my life likes F1 very much," she said.

She'd put it on and nothing else for their Skype call. And buy one for Anderson—no, he couldn't wear it since Nautilus sponsored another team. "I'll take two."

The man's wiry, white eyebrows shot up in surprise but it didn't stop him from getting to the cash register in Formula One speed. "Watching the race in the early hours, ma'am? Or will you wait 'til later to catch the highlights?"

"Oh I'll be up watching it."

He nodded approvingly. "Me, too. Let's see him beat that Yank this year."

Cass nodded emphatically. She couldn't have put it better herself. Buoyed by this experience, she swung the bag in her hand as she strolled down the swanky end of Bond Street. The sun even decided to come out, and it caught the polished, glazed surfaces of shop fronts and pillar boxes. A bronze statue gleamed in browns and yellows in front of a Rolex shop, a life-size bench called "the Allies," she learned as she drew closer, with realistic statues of Churchill and Roosevelt sitting on it. They looked to be having a scintillating conversation. A gap between them proved large enough to accommodate one other person. A gaggle of Chinese schoolgirls stood in front, taking turns to sit down between the bronze statesmen and pretend to hug either one of them as the others took photos. Cass grinned at the sight. Then she had a mad idea.

Dashing back to the shop, she arrived breathless.

The man raised his brows.

"Give me two more."

His hand reached into the case.

"Supernova this time."

His hand froze inside the glass cabinet. "You sure, ma'am?"

She grinned wickedly. "Oh, I'm sure."

She ran to the bench; the schoolgirls nowhere in sight. She fished out Ronan's tie from her bag, knotted it loosely around her own neck—it took her three tries to get right—then lifted it from her nape and draped it around Churchill's neck, obscuring his own crumpled bronze bow-tie. She repeated the procedure with the Supernova tie and put it on the Roosevelt sculpture.

She took a photo, and walked on ahead.

After a few yards she turned back to admire her handiwork and saw two suited gentlemen stop, fish out their phones, and take photos of the statues. She sent the photo to Ronan as she walked back toward the shops.

Ronan's reply was almost instantaneous. "Pressure from the top? I have to win now! Thanks so much."

Now she had a mission. She had to find another statue. Maybe a donkey for her remaining Maddux tie.

• • •

Ronan won that Sunday night, leaving Maddux second. Cass sat in bed, playing her own drinking game, cheering and taking a sip from her glass every time he managed to get the lead. The race had been nerve-rackingly close until the final pit stop where Ronan gained a few milliseconds. She wanted to run up and sink her body into him as he stood waiting to get on the podium, looking exhausted but exhilarated. Maddux, obviously caught in an off-guarded moment by a cameraman, looked thoroughly disgusted. His gaze caught the camera then, and he adjusted his features into a grin. The Texan did not have a poker face.

It took until after breakfast before she could talk to Ronan. She looked a total mess and was desperate for sleep now. Luckily, he looked equally wrecked.

"Are you up partying?" she asked.

"Kind of," he said sheepishly. "It's the Japanese. You have a moral obligation to go out; you wouldn't believe the pressure to drink."

"Good for you."

He peered into the camera. "And you? Did you see what that Churchill action has done?"

"What?"

"It's gone viral. Benny told me. Look at any social media site. They're mad about it. It's been tweeted tens of thousands of times apparently. It's been on the news in the States, even here in Nagoya."

"Is that so?" She didn't follow social media. Here was the proof it was as bewilderingly random as she'd always suspected. "Is that good?"

"Of course it is," he said. "My sponsors love it. The more publicity the better, especially when I win."

"Oh. Well, it was fun. And it seemed to have brought you luck."

"Now, Cass Miller, you don't believe that claptrap, do you?"

"No." She blew him a kiss. "But you do."

•••

Cass scoured the Internet for statues in London that were small enough to wrap a tie around and iconic enough to make a story. It was so much more enjoyable than exploring some musty, old museum just for the sake of it. And she ended up seeing more out-of-the-way spots and meeting more locals than she ever would have by following the guidebooks. She wanted one tie for each of the two races left in Asia, but soon she found herself traipsing back to that little F1 shop to buy more because so many lovely statues had presented themselves as perfect candidates. There was no reason she couldn't adorn them even when he wasn't racing. The shop owner greeted her with the kind of smile she expected he reserved for Queen Elizabeth herself.

"I've sold twenty of them in the last two days," he said. "Had to make an emergency order."

"So there are none left?"

He shook his head sadly. "But come back on Wednesday, ma'am."

"I will."

•••

"How the hell did you manage to climb up the Duke of Wellington statue?" Ronan asked the next night, from Kuala Lumpar. "I know that statue. You'd need a ladder to reach his neck."

"I did have a ladder."

He shook his head on the monitor. "Explain."

"I was looking up at it, minding my own business, and this group of guys came over and asked me if I was the Ronan Hawes tie girl—"

"The Ronan Hawes tie girl?"

"So I said yes. And they ran off to get me a ladder … without even asking."

"And then you got one of them to climb up and tie it, right?"

"Of course not, I climbed myself. It wouldn't be the same if I didn't do it."

He groaned. "You could've broken your neck. It's like, five meters high or something."

"Four and a half. And you sound like my mother. You realize I've had to climb ladders to check the helicopter, right?"

Ronan exhaled. "I give up. So did you at least get a wander in the park after that?"

"I walked through it to get to the Tube, yeah."

"The Tube? Sounds like you're really settling in, Cass."

"I am." And it was true. For the first night in a long time, she hadn't needed to touch the bourbon. She'd slept soundly last night, too.

Chapter 11

Ronan stood on a bridge surveying the unique Venice cityscape in the hazy dusk; the timeworn buildings that seem to float on water, and the marble steps that descended into lapping, teal waters. How serene. What a contrast to the past four weeks in sweltering hot Nagoya, Kuala Lumpar, and Shanghai with a meager one-out-of-three wins to show for it. A sharp longing to be with Cass had cut through his euphoria in Japan By the time he'd lost in China, watching her talking about putting those damn ties on statues was the only thing keeping him from falling into despair. She'd given him hope and kept his spirits up by showing him how loyal his British fans were. How loyal she was.

The distance had only amplified his lust for her, and his concern. He'd arrived in Venice a day earlier than she so he could adjust to the jet lag from the Singapore flight. She'd taken the Eurostar yesterday from England, and had been all day on a train down from Brussels today, due to arrive in two hours' time. He couldn't wait to see her expression when he escorted her to the gondola he'd ordered for 10:00 P.M. complete with gondolier and chilled champagne. She hadn't been many places outside the United States since her childhood, and he was excited to experience Venice with someone who hadn't been there, done that. Many of the women he'd dated had been as well travelled as he, and there was nothing new under the sun for them. There was only one little, black spot on the immediate horizon, and that was what he was about to do now. *If* he had the guts. One phone call. How hard could it be? He had to know what he was dealing with before the press did; information was power. Information meant being able to anticipate the next question before it caught him in deer-in-headlights mode at the next press conference for the world to see. And this was the only way. He sighed and looked around for somewhere quiet, somewhere far away from the chattering Chinese tourists who seemed to have accompanied his every step of the way since Shanghai.

A café beckoned, a typically understated affair with two rickety tables in front of a ridiculously quaint stone house with shutters. He ordered espresso from a matronly Italian woman. Telling himself he needed the caffeine to get through this, he gulped it down in two. Twisting around the empty cup on the saucer again and again, he pulled out his phone and stared at the Google logo on the screen. He searched for Springhill Prison contact details and stored the number under the name "Harry Hawes." The two were synonymous in his mind. How to address him after ten years? Dad, still? Ronan gritted his teeth and ordered another espresso, to the matron's delight. This would be the perfect time for a stiff drink if he were a drinker.

"Pull yourself together, Hawes," he muttered and pressed his thumb on the contact button. He leaned back in his chair and let his eyes wander over the tranquil alley scene playing out in front of him as the ring tone sounded. An Eastern European female voice answered. "Springhill Prison. How may I help you?" she said in a bored tone. The irony that he was calling Harry from Italy when the prison was less than an hour's drive from Silverstone didn't escape him. Neither did the fact that he and Cass had actually driven past it on their way to Danesfield House last month.

"I'd like to speak to Harry Hawes, please."

"We cannot allow direct calls, sir. You must give us your number, and Mr. Hawes will then call you back on a prison phone. The call will be traced for security and safety purposes."

"Yeah," said Ronan, frowning. He hadn't expected this. He didn't want to give Harry his number. God forbid. He glanced around the dark crevasses of the café to see if there was by any miracle a public phone. Of course not.

"Er, could you hang on a minute?" he asked.

There was a bit of whispering and muttering on the other end of the line. Not very professional at all. "Of course, sir," came the voice, a good deal more animated than before.

"Actually, I'll call you back, okay?" he said. They probably had his number on file now, but they wouldn't give it to Harry, would they?

He peered around again and caught his waitress's attention. "Um, signora?"

She bustled over, flapping her apron over and back in her haste to reach to the table. "*Signore?*"

"You have a telephone? Uh … *avete un telefono?*"

The woman's plump face squeezed together in pleasure. "*Telefono? Ma, naturalemente, signore!*"

She motioned impatiently for him to stand up, which he did. She grasped his forearm and all but pulled him to the back of the café where, indeed, a heavy, old, black telephone from the seventies sat on the counter.

"*Numero? Il numero?*"

She regarded him with blank, brown eyes, a crisscross of worry lines etched in her broad, tanned forehead.

"You see, I'll need them," Ronan gestured to the world outside the door, "to call me." He prodded his chest and then pointed to the phone. "To call this phone here."

Another blank look, and he fought the urge to groan. His Italian didn't stretch this far. Damn Harry and his stupid prison. They could all go to hell; he didn't have time for this.

"*Numero de … di … telefono?*" he tried again.

"*Ah … ah … signore!*" The penny had dropped. The waitress wrote down the number on a beermat, in painfully slow, ridiculously large digits. "*E questo, e questo.*" She held it up to him as if he had to inspect it for correctness or something. He took it from her fingers, nodding. "*Grazie.*"

Pleasure flooded into her face again. He smiled back, just long enough to show his gratitude, short enough to hint that he needed a little privacy now. It was unnecessary, as she bustled off of her own accord. He heaved a sigh and dialed the prison again, using the funny, old-fashioned dial that clicked at every revolution. He'd never used an old phone before.

"Springhill Prison. How may I help you?" rattled off the same Eastern European female voice.

"Yeah, hi, I just called. I'm looking for—"

"Oh, yes, sir, yes, sir." The voice hitched up to a girlish tone. He heard scuffling. A pause. He shook his head in disbelief.

"Springhill Prison," came a male voice, somewhat shaky. "How may I help you?"

"Yes, I'm looking for Harry Hawes."

"I see. And may I take your name please?"

"I'm …" Ronan hesitated. "I'm his son. Ronan Hawes. I believe you'll need a number for him to call me, so I can give that to you now." He held up the beermat and squinted at the numbers in the semi-darkness.

"Yes, Mr. Hawes. And can I say it's an honor and a pleasure to talk to you."

"Uh, you're welcome?" Ronan could hear his voice echoing. He was on speakerphone. Jesus, this prison, what was it? A kindergarten? He heard someone saying something like "It *is* him. It *is* him!"

"Okay, so, here's the number then—"

"I watched you on Sunday, Mr. Hawes. So impressive. We're all fans here at Springhill, you know …" A chorus of mumbles sounded through the line. How many people were listening to this?

"Thanks, thanks very much." Ronan pressed a hand to his forehead and dragged it down his face. "Could I … just … talk to my father, please?"

"Yes, of course, Ronan … I mean Mr. Hawes." Another round of smothered chuckles. "Erm, please call out the number there and we'll call you back in a jiffy, sir."

Ronan read out the string of digits through gritted teeth.

"Plus thirty three. That's Italy," said the prison officer, with some uncertainty.

"Y-e-e-s," said Ronan, patiently.

"But your next race is Texas."

"Uh-huh. Correct."

"Forgive me, Mr. Hawes. You'll hear presently from your father. Please wait. Please note that the call will be traced—"

"For security and safety reasons. Got it." No doubt it would be traced for fandom reasons now, too, and played on YouTube for posterity if he wasn't lucky.

"Goodbye, Mr. Hawes … and good luck in Texas, sir! You show that Texan!"

"Thank you, I certainly intend to." Ronan all but slammed down the receiver with a heavy clunk and sat watching it. His gaze wandered to the waitress, who was busy outside talking to an old guy. She spun around with the sixth sense of all good waitresses and caught his eye.

"Espresso, signore?"

He shook his head. Another of those and he'd be wired to the big pink moon now ascending over the canal outside. She returned to her conversation on the patio, leaving Ronan alone with his dark memories.

"Come on, old man," he hissed at the phone. Then it rang.

"Hello?" Ronan said, a lot shakier than he liked.

"Who's this?" came the waspish voice he immediately recognized. Dad. Ronan stopped himself exclaiming it just in time. A single memory of his father putting his first karting trophy on the mantelpiece came shooting back. "It—it's me, Ronan. Didn't they tell you?"

A silence. How long Ronan couldn't judge.

"Ronan?" The voice was unstable now. "Or just some bastard messing with me? They said it was Italy. My son's not in Italy."

"Well, actually, he is. It is me."

"Prove it."

"Don't you recognize my voice?"

A raspy sigh. "It could be you, son, but this kind of thing has happened before."

It had? Jesus. And had he been fooled? Ronan's gut tightened.

Specificity was the key, but all he could think of was the general hurt he was experiencing, the shame and the grief he and his mother had suffered because of this man's criminal legacy. He sighed. "Remember the shelf you built for my second trophy when I was nine, and you busted your index finger with the hammer on the last nail? Because I do." Harry hadn't complained either. Had just walked away in agony and covered the pain with big smiles all evening. The memory still brought a warm heavy feeling to Ronan's chest.

"Son! It is you!" Harry gave an old man's chuckle followed by a wheeze that Ronan had never heard before. He'd aged in voice anyway. What did he look like now?

"Are they letting you out?"

Harry exhaled loudly into the receiver. "Guess so, son. November. The twenty-fourth to be precise, if I can trust the buggers. You getting ready with the red carpet?" he asked, warily.

"No. I just need to know." Ronan kept his tone even. "I'm sure you can look after yourself." *As you always do.*

"Don't you worry about your old man, my lad. You've got enough to be concentrating on. Good job in Silverstone. I know you always wanted to win there."

Ronan winced at the truth of this and gritted his teeth tighter, determined not to get sucked in.

"And I know you're going for champion. I can tell by the way you're playing the press and giving it your all. You will get it this year; I can feel it. That Maddux guy can shove his energy drink up his arse!"

Ronan laughed, despite himself. And then hated himself for giving Harry this advantage.

"That's my boy." Harry sounded quite animated now. "You'll do it. Do it for all those years you've worked up to this moment."

"Yes. Well. Not quite there yet," Ronan cut in before Harry could take some of the credit for himself. "I need to keep my head clear, and I need you to stay out of trouble when you get out." Had he spoken to his father like his before? Probably not. It felt good. "Look, just lay low. After Hockenheim, I don't care. But before that, stay out of the press. Can you do that?"

"My boy, I'd give anything … anything … my life itself … to see you champion. You know that."

The blood drained from Ronan's face. This wasn't going the way he'd expected. "Fine. Bye then." He hung up and sank back into an uncomfortable wooden chair nearby. He didn't notice the matron until she was right up at the table, her huge bosom alarmingly near his face. "No, *signora*, no more espresso, *grazie*."

• • •

The Venice Mestre train station was crowded as usual, but Cass was on time; he didn't have to wait long in the throng of tourists before her smiling face appeared like an apparition before him on platform five. She sank into his hug, and the tension drained out of his body.

"Nearly didn't recognize you with the cap and shades," her muffled voice vibrated against his chest.

"That's the general idea." Ronan peered around and saw a clear getaway with no potential F1 fans blocking it. "This way; no time to lose." She pulled out from his embrace, eyes alight. "Before what?"

"You'll see." He smiled and hitched her suitcase over his shoulder. Always a light traveller, Cass. It had been the same for their overnighter in Danesfield House—just one compact suitcase. Vivienne used to mobilize half a store's worth of Louis Vuitton cases for the shortest of trips, all color-coordinated, though how her skimpy costumes amassed to such a volume he could never figure out.

"Oh, a surprise?" Her tone made it plain she wasn't a fan of them. Well, she'd like this.

• • •

The water taxi trundled across the Laguna Veneta. She couldn't take her eyes off the splendor of the scene. He leaned back, inhaling the breeze and enjoying her rapt expression. They could've taken the train, but he wanted to experience her first impression of Venice from the water, the proper way.

"Let's dump the bag later," he suggested, "And go straight to the surprise."

Anxiety creased her forehead. "It doesn't involve flying, does it?"

"Nope, just more water." The boat came to a standstill, and he led her out. She was wearing boots without much heel. Good. Venice did not treat stilettos kindly.

Cass was staring at the gondolas lined up against the promenade.. "This is exactly how I imagined Venice. Are we actually going to go in one of these?"

"Yes, if I can find Piero," Ronan said, scanning the row of eager gondoliers. "Ah. There he is—in the pink shirt behind the lamp post."

"Are you sure it's okay with the bag?" Cass frowned at the brown bag by his feet on the cobblestones.

He threw an arm over her shoulders. "Would you stop worrying?"

"Sorry." She grinned and squeezed his hand. "I'll try. I mean, if I can't relax here—"

"*Buena sera*," intoned a jovial voice. A weather-beaten Italian man slid up to them, shooing away some younger gondola drivers blocking the pier. "Signore Ronan and his lovely lady." He looked Cass up and down in the appreciative way that only Italians seemed to get away with. Cass snorted into her chiffon scarf. "*Prego*, come down." Piero waved them down impatiently.

Ronan stepped down the timeworn granite steps and took her hand to guide her into the gently rocking gondola. The suitcase was deposited on the spare seat. He leaned back on the plush red velvet and pulled her back with him. "Piero, *amico mio*, let's drive this baby!"

"Faster than you, *signore*, in Abu Dhabi." Piero's wizened face twisted in hilarity.

"He would remember the close race I lost recently," Ronan murmured into Cass's ear. "I'll ignore him. I suggest you do likewise." He slid his arm under her jacket, fingering for an opening in her blouse to touch her skin, realizing how hungry he was for her, and almost—almost—wishing he hadn't prepared a surprise and had just dragged her to the hotel room. With his other hand he pulled the champagne out of the ice bucket. Finding he couldn't actually open it with one hand, he sighed and pushed it back into the bucket again. His other arm slid under her jacket, too. She yelped and bolted upright. "God, that's cold!" She slapped him off. "Your hands are like ice!"

Piero laughed and thrust the oar into the water, and they were off, gently rocking. Ronan remembered the previous times he'd been here, same boat, Piero's regular forward strokes each followed by a compensating backward stroke. They'd become friendly a few years back when Ronan had to endure an advertisement filming, repeating a gondola trip fourteen times until the director was happy. Piero had introduced him to a real Italian café with lovely people afterward, and effectively rescued him from the tiresome film crew.

Ronan's body pressed against Cass's as the gondola bobbed along the gray-green water, lights sparkling from streetlamps and windows all reflected hazily in the river. He kicked off his shoes and sighed. "Let the good times roll." He loved watching the familiar bustle at the banks of the Grand Canal and observing Cass as she saw everything for the first time. She actually "ooh-ed" when they went under their first bridge. He gave her another minute of sightseeing before twisting to her again. "Now, where were we?" She giggled as he slid his hands against her midriff and gently squeezed. Maybe he shouldn't have bothered with the gondola. He was having trouble keeping his hands off her. He needed to get her back to a room. Now.

She darted a look at Piero, who ignored them and lit up a cigarette. She nudged Ronan's shin with her foot. "Open this champagne."

Ronan expertly popped the cork. "What'll we toast to?" he asked as he clinked his glass against hers. He loved how her face glowed in the dusk, and how gentleness had replaced the brittle anxiety.

"Next race?"

"Us," he said softly.

"So ... where are we going?"

"No clue," he said. "I just told Piero to keep it tranquil and as far away from other tourists as possible. He's one of the best, knows the canal system like the back of his hand. So don't worry."

"I'm not worried about him, I'm more worried about you. Look, your glass nearly went in."

"Oops." He grabbed the champagne flute that he'd perched on the edge of the boat. "Don't worry, we drivers have lightning sharp reflexes. I'd have caught it before it fell in."

"Lightning sharp, huh?" she said. "Well what if I were to throw this?" She held up his Italian moccasin shoe.

"Hey." He sat up. "Watch it, they're my favorite shoes."

"But you'd catch it, if I were to say … drop it?" Her hand hovered over the side of the gondola, the shoe dangling from her long finger.

"You do and I'll—"

"What?" she challenged, "Come and get it, Tiger."

He stretched across her, deliberately pressing his weight against her, and whipped the shoe from her hand. "I hope you can swim."

She laughed. "Of course. But you wouldn't dare."

Without thinking, he pinned her back with his left arm and slid his right arm up her thigh before she could react. Her A-line skirt made it easy, and her lounging position on the bench even easier, to whip down the soft, slinky material of her underwear. Her knee jerked up violently, just missing his face, but he grabbed it into him and tugged the lacy garment over her shoeless feet. She fought him, laughing, but he sank back, victoriously holding the clutch of teal blue silk in the breeze. It looked familiar. Did she buy them in six packs? A glance at Piero showed he had his back to them, giving them a modicum of privacy.

Cass lunged for the underwear, but Ronan held it closer to his chest. "Mine."

"Is that so?" She bent down to grab his shoe. He'd left himself open for that bad tactical move. He narrowed his eyes at her. "What do you think you're doing?" As if in slow motion, he saw her shoulder flexing and the telltale stiffening of her biceps as she prepared to fling the shoe. He bolted forward, catching the shoe just as it left her hand, and experienced a moment of triumph as it left her grip and slid into his. But then something wasn't right, the center of gravity had somehow shifted and he wasn't landing in the boat, he was … going over the edge, water coming toward him, deep gray water …

He yelped as he submerged. Memories of childhood swims in the freezing Atlantic whipped back, and then a blank slate of shock. Painfully cold. Shit. How filthy was this water anyway? He resurfaced, gasping and grappling at the slimy wooden side of the gondola. No grips. He backed off to get a better look. Cass and Piero were staring at him, white faced, both comically round-eyed. Then Cass's hand went to her mouth and she let out a yelp of laughter. Piero joined in, his baritone guffaws cascading as Cass's receded.

"Bloody hell, help me out here, you bastards!" he called, spitting out a mouthful of briny water. Cass and Piero held out their arms in unison and he grappled for one of each. Then he had a better idea. He let go of Piero's and tugged Cass's arm until she, too, went toppling over the edge with an ear-piercing scream.

She scrambled to the surface and shrieked again. "Oh my God, you asshole!" She started a front crawl to the edge of the water to some stone steps. He followed her, admiring her quick thinking and the speed she kept up. He'd never swum with clothes on before. Where was his mobile phone? Wallet? No, they were in his jacket on the boat. Thank God.

She clambered up onto the stone steps in front of him, her wet skirt clearly revealing her lack of anything on underneath. Despite everything else his body was telling him, the sight of her shivering contours in that translucent, wet cotton skirt thickened his blood. He pulled himself out of the water and followed her up the steps, squelching. She sat huddled on a low wall, wringing out a mass of dripping hair. "Oh my God, I can't believe you did that," she panted. "You're just evil."

"You started it," he said, heaving. He let out a snicker that turned into helpless laughter. She whipped around and her face crumbled into mirth as well, her white teeth flashing under the streetlights before she bent forward to clutch her stomach. He continued laughing, now more out of surprise and relief at her reaction. She couldn't seem to stop.

She sat up gasping and looked him up and down.

"What're you looking at? You're every bit as wet as I am."

"I know." Her smile was incandescent.

His breath caught in his chest. Her smiles were rare, but when they came, they illuminated her right through to her soul, and he was lost. What had she been like before the accident? He imagined times like this, seeing her helpless with laughter. The camera capturing her exuberance when she told him about putting the ties on the statues were what the old Cass had been like. Before the guilt of the accident overwhelmed her.

"What?" He held out his dripping arms and pulled his hands in again to wipe more gunk off his face.

"Sorry?" she offered, looking far from contrite.

He shook his head. "My fault, I guess." He glanced around instinctively for a taxi, but of course there were none. No cars at all. Just people, tourists, and cameras flashing. Cameras … flashing. Damn. He turned instinctively toward the river and tugged Cass close. "Don't turn to them," he said. "We've to go back down." He led the way back to the water. Bless him, Piero was ready and waiting with the gondola right up against the steps. "*Signore*, quick."

Ronan jumped in and turned to catch Cass. They flumped down on the ornate bench again, their collective wetness seeping into the velvet. Piero whipped around and threw them two blankets. "Quick," he said with a vaguely circular motion of his hands. Ronan draped one around Cass. She was shaking as much as he was, but she smiled up at him sheepishly. "Get us to our hotel as quickly as possible, but if you know a secret way, all the better," he called to Piero.

"No problem." Piero was talking into a phone. "My son ... he will come now. With motorboat, yes?"

Cass clung to her blanket as they waited for the motorboat to arrive. She'd noticed Ronan checking his watch three times in the past minute, his expression growing somber. Piero had smoked two cigarettes in succession and shot them mixed looks of sympathy and incredulity between drags.

"What's up?" she asked Ronan finally. "Worried about catching a cold? I actually understand that now—how important it is for a driver to be on peak fitness, especially in the neck region—"

"I'm fine." Ronan turned his head back to the pier where the gaggle of journalists had dispersed.

"Oh, The press." She was definitely back in his crazy world, the one where they were on stage all the time.

The Skype chats with him, though frequent, had retained a sheen of the intangible. But here he was solidly physical, and the freezing water had awakened her body and her mind from the haze she'd drifted into while in London. Woken her—to him. To who he really was. A man who cared about others. About her.

. He pulled her in tightly to his side. Within seconds they heard the drone of a motorboat approaching.

"Tonio," called Piero, lifting his oar in greeting to his nephew. Tonio was a younger version of Piero except his shock of hair was black instead of gray.

"Thank Christ," muttered Ronan, standing up. She jumped up, too, and tried to control her shivering as they jumped from the gondola into the much bigger—and warmer—interior of the motorboat. The resourceful nephew had brought soup in a Thermos, an assortment of towels, and a heap of dry clothes. He waved at them to make themselves comfortable and started the engine. Ronan handed a wad of Euros to Piero and shook his hand before dashing inside to the warmth.

"What did you say to him?" she asked, handing him a large towel.

"Oh, just that you're crazy and that you threw me in the water."

"Come on, let's get off these wet things or we will get hyperthermia. I feel guilty already about risking your health here."

"And so you should."

She'd got him joking again, but his expression remained tense the whole way back to the pier where they were to get off. Even changing into the ersatz clothing Tonio had provided didn't bring on a fit of laughter from him like it normally would. He looked comical in jeans that were too wide and too short. Luckily she could take her own clothes from her luggage. She chose the warmest things she'd packed—jeans and a sweater. She teased him about his new Italian look, but all it induced from him, as they crossed the picturesque Rialto Market square, was a terse, "We're a fine pair to be walking into the Ca' Sagredo Hotel."

Chapter 12

As it turned out, the staff at the Ca' Sagredo Hotel didn't bat an eyelid, as if guests in ill-fitting clothing with damp, canal-scented hair were only to be expected. This inscrutability simply compounded the magic of the truly high-end hotel experience. It certainly had its advantages. Ronan ordered room service; she was ravenous. Eating five-star food might just curb her longing for a nice, warming, double shot of bourbon. And then he ran the tub, and the vanilla of the bubble bath wafted like an elixir into her sinuses.

"We smell gross," she said.

"No kidding." Ronan turned the taps to full blast and straightened. "We smell like Supernova."

She smiled, stripping off the jeans, with nothing on underneath. That got his immediate attention. "Not sure I can let you go long enough to have a bath," he murmured, advancing in two quick steps.

She pushed against his chest playfully. "You can wash my hair if you'd like."

Ronan smiled back but then sat down on the bed saying, "No, you go ahead. I'll stay out here in case room service arrives."

Room service wouldn't arrive for at least another ten minutes at the quickest. She spied his outline through the translucent glass door of the bathroom, sitting motionless on the bed where she'd left him. He wasn't himself. Something was bugging him, and she was going to find out what it was—after his shower and his food. Maybe it was just the jet lag. Or the losses in Asia.

Thirty minutes later she sat opposite him, wrapped in a sumptuous, white terrycloth dressing gown.

"You okay?"

Ronan, hair still wet from his shower, looked up from his barbecued ribs. "Mmm-hmm."

"Glad to be back in Europe?"

His eyebrows shot up. "Are you kidding? I couldn't wait to get back." He gestured with the bone in his hand. "To you, to this kind of food, to a week off from the grind, to everything."

"You seemed happier before."

"No, you're wrong." Ronan put down the bone on his plate, and picked at it with a knife. "Winning Japan—" he shook his head "—was incredible. But the Malaysia and China races killed me. Mechanical issues, as you've probably heard. I didn't even make it to the podium."

"You'll catch up."

"Maddux and Supernova are pulling away. I can feel it."

"I know your second two races were a bummer, but you have to be happy with how your teammate did."

"Yeah, Mitchell's saving our team right now, but Bates ... oh, how I'd love to kick his ass all over his own turf."

She smiled. "I'd like to see that."

Ronan fisted his hand around his knife. "I just have to manage to not screw it up in Texas and then Hockenheim. Two races; that's it."

"You won't screw it up, Ronan."

"I know. I can't. I can't let anything distract me."

"Like?"

Wait. Was he talking about her? Her heart lurched. "Is this the 'it's not you, it's me' speech?" she asked, struggling to keep her tone even. She swallowed, hard, reaching for her water.

"What? No, no, nothing like that."

"Then what? Seriously, Ronan, spill. I'm getting worried here."

Something—annoyance, anxiety—crossed his face, drawing his cheek muscles inward. "Remember that news article about my father?"

"Getting out of prison, yes."

"Well, his release isn't far away now."

"Ah."

"Yeah," he said.

"Well, I mean, they're letting him out, but he's not coming to live with you or anything."

"It's enough that he's in the news. It's going to hit me, too. Big time."

"Can't you just ignore it?"

"No."

"But—"

"No, Cass. I'm his son, goddamn it. They won't let me forget him."

"They? The press?"

He nodded.

She'd seen one or two mentions of Harry Hawes in the British press while staying at Dad's apartment, but she thought the coverage from Asia would have obliterated all interest in his father's misdeeds. Apparently Ronan didn't think so.

"What's the best way to play it?" she asked.

"I'm not playing it any way," he growled. "He can go to hell as far as I'm concerned."

She opened her mouth to reply but he held up his hand. "I can't discuss this."

"Can't or won't?"

"Won't. Not here. Not now. Not ever. Sorry."

She let his words hang there as they finished their meal. She'd touched a nerve, an incredibly raw nerve, just like he'd touched several of hers these past few weeks they'd known each other. Experience with her own personal anguish made it tempting to just leave well enough alone, to let him deal with it on his own terms in his own time. And yet, it was eating away at him now. He wasn't someone who could hide what was going on underneath.

And she found herself wanting to know what was going on underneath.

Fuck it. I'm going to try again.

"Will you see him when he gets out?" she asked, stirring her tea as if they'd just moved onto a completely new topic.

Ronan raised his eyes. His stormy expression rooted her to her seat, but she held his gaze firmly.

"You could just go there, pick him up, and deposit him in some hotel somewhere. I'd come with you if you'd want."

His look was one of pure astonishment now. Not the good kind. Before he could explode, she added, "Yes, I know it'll be bad timing just before Hockenheim, and you certainly don't need the distraction, but maybe not doing it could be even worse?" She gave him her most matter-of-fact smile to cover up her nervousness. "I mean, you can just picture the headlines, can't you? 'F1 Star Abandons Ailing Seventy-year-old Father Released from Prison,' accompanied by image of pitiful old man trudging the dirt track outside Springhill, alongside a colorful photo of you guzzling champagne with an F1 babe."

Ronan's rigidity seemed to relax a fraction but his deep frown remained in place before he said caustically, "The F1 babe would be you, remember? Well, I can see another headline, 'Get Out of Jail Fast,' and a cartoon with him and me in the car, accompanied by full backstory of his misdeeds, trying to induce some parallels between our lives. Jesus, as if there were any!"

Cass touched his hand lightly.

He flinched.

She drew back. "Sorry. Just do what you think will cause you the least soul searching later on; what you feel is right."

He shrugged.

"Just don't let it consume you."

He cocked an eyebrow. "Fine words, Cass. Fine words. But maybe you should take your own advice."

She looked down quickly, busying herself with squeezing the tea bag on her saucer.

"Cass—"

"It's okay, Ronan." Blood pounded in her ears. Was he going to throw this back on her every time she tried to help him? "You think I'm having issues? Well, I am. Someone *died* thanks to me. I'm just doing the best I can here, all right?"

Ronan's expression, when he raised his eyes to hers again, had softened with contrition. "I'm sorry. Truly. But I also think you need to put it in perspective."

She laughed, humorlessly. "How's that?"

"Lots of people have lived, thanks to you."

She froze, teacup halfway to her mouth.

"All those people on highways, the people who needed transport to a better hospital? You saved plenty and lost one. I'm sorry I was flippant just now." He stood, reached out, and tugged her arm until she had to put down the cup and stand up, too. He took two paces back and flumped back onto the bed, pulling her down with him, with her back facing him, staring straight ahead.

"Said I was sorry, Cass. I was just, I don't know, trying to put it in perspective." He sat up, trailed his hand down her spine, reached the almost-ticklish spot above her hip bone, and circled his finger there, as she looked over her shoulder at him.

"I don't see it that way." She wanted to stop talking, to stop thinking, to shut out the world and spend a week alone with this man on a different planet. His father issue was nothing she could fix, but she could at least help distract him as he had helped her.

"I know," he said.

Gradually she relaxed. She slid down, the small of her back resting on his thighs as she gazed up into his face, his expression thoughtful Her fingers trailed lazily into the opening of his dressing gown and along his midriff, and his whole abdomen clenched. He responded by ripping open her robe and placing his palms on her belly. Her lips relaxed, urging him silently to sink his mouth onto hers, which he did with a crushing intensity. "I'm going to pleasure you," he growled, coming out of the long kiss, smoothing one hand down until his fingertips reached her pubic bone, and the other hand up between her breasts. Yeah, this was the one thing they could definitely do for each other.

Chapter 13

The loudspeaker announced their flight to New York, continuing on to Texas, would be boarding in ten minutes. Thank God she'd stocked her purse with mini-bottles of liquor from the gift shop. Cass pulled the third one from her purse and downed the contents. Ronan glanced over from his seat next to her.

"Okay there?" he asked.

"I will be. She washed the vodka down with a mouthful of fizzy imported water. "Some pilot, huh?"

He stroked a hand through her hair.

"It should keep me from freaking out on you. But if it doesn't—."

"It will. I'm sure plenty of people have had panic attacks on planes. Maybe you should consider talking to someone—a doctor," he added hastily as she opened her mouth to speak.

Here we go again with the "talk to someone" suggestion. People always wanted her to admit she wasn't able to cope. No thanks. Time was all she needed. But it wasn't getting better. Shouldn't it be getting better by now? She fished in her bag for another bottle. "Self-medicating is working." Where were those damn bottles?

He covered her frantically searching hand with his and withdrew it from the cavernous bag.

"I'll take care of you" After their discussion in the hotel, she thought they'd come to an implicit agreement to lay off the difficult topics. She didn't need this on top of flying. Her heartbeat picked up. "Uh, Ronan? Best if we talk about something else," she said pointedly. "How 'bout that Texas race?" "Or how my season is shot to hell?" he said.

She squeezed his hand. OK, another bad topic. The alcohol was kicking in. Leaving her pleasantly buzzed, relaxed enough to fly, or so she hoped. "And you're sure this is okay? Traveling with me, instead of with the team?"

"They don't care how we get there, only that we do. And, frankly, I'm sick of all the strategizing and second-guessing. In Texas they're going to try," he glanced around, but she already knew no one was watching, "some new tech in the car."

"What kind of new tech?"

He linked his fingers together and stared at them. "I can't say. It's proprietary stuff. But it could give me an edge for my last two races this year. And when I tested it in the preseason, the benefits were significant out of the turns."

"So why isn't it in the car?"

"There was some … trouble with the testing."

That got her attention. "What kind of trouble?" she asked, suspiciously.

"It wasn't ready, but it is now. The engineers have been working on it 'round the clock and they're going to install it. It'll give me an advantage out there, you'll see."

"Is it safe?"

He sent her a half smile. "Safe is relative in this sport, but if they hadn't worked out the issues, they wouldn't chance it."

"Legal or loophole?" Anderson had explained that rules and regulations governed nearly all aspects of the car, and compliance with the rules was routinely, vigorously checked. If anything was amiss, any rules violated, drivers were penalized. But there were loopholes, and the teams were brilliant at exploiting them—it was part of the reason for the changes every season.

"Does it matter? Probably legal. We all know it's now or never for me, Cass."

She put her hand across his hands, now tightly clenched together. Two more races.

They called for first class passengers to board. She'd be home before she knew it. Maybe it was the alcohol, maybe Ronan, but she couldn't summon any feelings on it as exhaustion took over.

She settled into the first-class seat, leaned her head back and closed her eyes. She felt the lift as the plane lumbered into the air, and that was her last thought.

• • •

Ronan looked over to her sleeping face beside him in the hotel bed, the best room Austin, Texas, had to offer—so relaxed, angelic almost.

Cassidy's cell phone rang, waking her up. "Sorry," she whispered to him before she answered with "Hello?" in a voice still thick with sleep.

He changed position, hoping to get another hour of sleep. The jet lag going to the States was awful for him. Every damn time. Worse than in the other direction.

The hotel mattress shifted, and the bathroom door closed a second later.

Why was she taking the call in the bathroom? He pushed away his suspicions. She wasn't Viv. She wasn't arranging the next relationship before the conclusion of the first.

Still.

He pushed the pillows to the headboard and sat up.

She opened the door to the bathroom, her expression stark.

"Tell me," he commanded.

"I need to go to EvacuAir in Surprise, Arizona, Monday."

No wonder she looked wretched. "What did they say?"

"They told me to bring all my gear." Her gaze was steady. She was pale, but calm. "We can still do my family's early Thanksgiving tomorrow. The headquarters is only two hours from my folks."

"What exactly does 'bring your gear' mean?"

She shot him a sardonic look. "It means you're fired; what did you think?"

"How much pull does the report have in the industry?"

She shrugged. "I don't know. I had an instructor who crashed flying tours, but I can't ask him, he's dead."

"Can they take away your license?"

"No, only the Federal Aviation Authority can do that. The FAA will see the internal company report, but it will base its recommendations on the final incident report filed by the National Transportation Safety Board—the completion of those investigations are months away."

"Surely they can't take your license permanently?"

She sat on the bed. "Ronan."

"I'm sorry. I'm not … I don't know what to say. I just want to fix it, or fight it or … or be prepared for it."

He reached for her hand and held it. "You've never really told me what happened."

"You never really asked. None of you have ever asked. Not Jim, not my mom, Anderson—no one. And I haven't talked about it since the investigation."

"Well I want to know."

Her hand slid away, and she positioned her body away from his, keeping her knee between them. "Do you really? Does it matter?" Her expression was stony.

"Cass. I'm a professional driver. Do you think I've never caused accidents? Never been responsible for injuring someone in my career? Of course I have. Other drivers get hurt and, at times, killed on the courses I race. I'm the last person, the very last person, who would ever judge you for making a mistake." He took her hand back and held it tightly. "Telling me what happened isn't going to change how I feel about you."

"Then why haven't you asked?"

"Because I wasn't sure talking about it was the best thing. And when I have asked about what you're going through, you shut me down. I don't have a lot of confidence in my ability to help you through something like this. I'm no good at … giving emotional support. I'm never sure what the best thing is with you. Talk about it? Ignore it?"

She stiffened.

"See? You get tense every time the subject comes up." He shrugged. "I … I've been quite happy swimming in the shallows—but you … you've thrust me into the deep end. And frankly, I'm not sure I can give you what you need. But I want to. I really want to."

"I appreciate that but …

"No buts. I want you to tell me."

"You know those things people say after you lose a race?"

It was his turn to stiffen. "Yeah."

"Those things like 'there's always the next race, always next year' and the like?"

"Yes."

"It's like that, Ronan. I don't want to hear platitudes. Not from you. I don't want you to tell me how I wasn't wrong or talk about fate or luck or how it could've happened to anyone. The decision I made, the wrong decision, got someone killed. And I don't know that I'll ever come to terms with it."

Her hands were shaking, her expression bleak.

"I would give anything, my life included, to have a chance to redo—"

"But—"

She held up a hand. "So before I tell you the specifics, you have to know there is nothing you or anyone else could say that can make what happened easier to bear." She stood. "Make coffee. I'll have a shower. And then I'll tell you about that night."

As he watched her retreat into the bathroom he finally understood what she was living through. And there wasn't a damn thing he could do about it.

•••

The hot water streamed over her shoulders. She couldn't put it off any longer. Of course he wanted to know. What he didn't want to know was that it had been her fault. He said it wouldn't make a difference, but it would. Dread crept through her. She wasn't even sure her family would still love her if they knew the details, and they were required to.

Telling Ronan the truth about the crash would be torture. He held real sway over her heart, and his negative reaction could crush her.

She turned off the water and wrapped herself in the oversized, plush, white towel. Ronan was on the phone when she came out. He was ordering breakfast from the half of the conversation she could hear. She dressed quickly. Now that she had made up her mind to tell him, she wanted to get it over with.

He handed her a cup of coffee and patted the sofa next to him. "I told room service to leave it outside the door."

"They'll get used to doing that," she said with an attempt at a smile. "So we got the call at 1:00 A.M., for an MVA—car accident. Single car, ran off the road, flipped a few times. Drunk, fell asleep, as it turned out."

"You landed on the highway, at night?"

She nodded.

"That alone sounds dangerous."

A shaky laugh escaped her. "Says the racecar driver."

"You've done a lot of those?"

"In my three years working EMS? Dozens. The difference this time was that we were supposed to get weather."

"Storms?"

"No, fog, low clouds. I check the forecast before we all go to bed—we sleep in a big trailer at the base, then I check again if we get a call. Besides the official sources for weather, I have three weather apps on my phone."

"Right."

"So the radar wasn't clear, but the direction we were going it looked to be okay. And that's all I really needed to know. We could always wait to come back to base. I took the call and woke my nurse, Julie, and Steve."

"The paramedic, right?" He stared at her. "Did you have feelings for him?" he asked.

"No. God, no. Nothing like that. I liked him. He was a good guy. A really good guy."

"Go on."

"It was a typical scene call. I put her down on the highway, no problems. The kid was in bad shape. Lots of fractures, internal injuries, and a punctured lung. They got him as stable as they could, and we got out of there."

"Did you help?"

"With treating him? No, that's not part of my job. The pilot doesn't do the medical stuff. I might carry things, but I don't help. We got the kid to the hospital; it was touch and go a few times. I've learned to tune all that out and just concentrate on flying. And my nurse and Steve were a good crew—they never panicked, argued, or freaked out in my headphones." She smiled. "They made a terrific team." Her smile disintegrated as she remembered how quiet things had gotten later that night.

"That leg was uneventful. I checked the weather again while they took him into the hospital. There were some clouds, but the radar looked good to go—I saw a few warnings about low lying clouds in the areas west of our path, but figured we had time. It was only an hour from the hospital to base."

There was a knock at the door.

"Leave it," Ronan called out.

She held her head in her hands, her heart racing. She willed away the panic with deep breaths, ignoring the fact that he was staring at her. After a moment, she continued. "So we headed back. Thirty minutes from base, I flew into a cloud."

That was the danger inherent with the night vision goggles. You could be flying along completely unaware you had reduced visibility and then bam! Blind.

"And that's when everything went wrong," she said.

"Don't you have instruments or—?"

"Yes. I'm instrument rated. We learn how to fly in the clouds wearing an opaque hood, but that's a whole other thing. Going suddenly into a no-visibility situation—there aren't instruments to tell you where the hills and trees and power lines and—anyway. So when it happens, there's a certain procedure you're supposed to follow. I didn't follow it."

"What did you do?" he asked, gently.

"I turned around, a 180-degree turn, back out the way I'd gone in. Pure instinct."

"And that's not what you're supposed to do?"

"No. There's a procedure for sudden loss of visibility due to weather—it's called an inadvertent instrument meteorological condition. I'm supposed to climb to a high enough altitude to be out of danger of obstacles, reach air traffic control to confess my problem, communicate understanding of their instructions, and comply with their guidance to the closest place to land—the four C's. It's drilled into us in training."

"Right, and instead you turned and headed out the way you came in, where you could see?"

"Thought I could see. And as it turned out, I could—initially. I could see enough to put her down. And then I couldn't. The ceiling was dropping fast, and I went for it. We were out in a remote area. Visibility was worse by the second. It was a good landing, a bit hard, but I didn't realize how unstable the ground was or that there was a slight elevation. It was night, difficult to see, even with goggles. I … I put down, and one skid wasn't stable, but I was already flipping everything off to prevent a fire—fire is the big danger, you see," she said, dully. "But the ground didn't hold under the skid. We flipped left, and that side of the aircraft was crushed. We slid, on our side, down the slope. It happened so fast. The rotors … and my medic was the only one …"

Ronan handed her a glass of water, and she took a sip.

"I pulled off my headphones; we had to get out."

He nodded.

"Julie was talking, so I was pretty sure she was okay, but Steve … he wasn't."

She covered her mouth. Was she going to be sick?

"He was in bad shape," she whispered, wrapping her arms around her abdomen, rocking. "That side of the aircraft had been crushed—crumpled …"

He attempted to put an arm around her, but she pulled away, shrinking into herself. "We managed to get him out—I don't like to think about it. He was in a lot of pain. After we dragged him a safe distance away, Julie went back and grabbed her kit, which was incredibly brave. He was … you have to understand; we've seen a lot of bad accidents, a lot of injuries. And we knew. He wasn't talking; he couldn't … just gasping. Julie started the IV and pushed pain meds."

"Did they help?"

"He died within minutes. I'd like to think the pain was easing when he died."

"He didn't say anything?"

"One of the things I learned on the job is that when people are dying, they don't have these profound things to say. They're in pain, or shock, and it's not like in the movies."

The tiny muscles around Ronan's eyes tightened, and he stared at her, not blinking for what seemed like a long time. Then he looked down at his hands. "Yes, yes, of course not—"

She pressed her palms together tightly, watching his reaction. "So now you know."

"It doesn't sound to me like you did anything that wrong."

"Ronan. I told you, the four C's."

"How do you know the outcome would've been any better?"

"I don't know anything for sure, but they have to fire me; they're right in firing me. I didn't follow protocol."

"What about your license?"

"No clue. Suspension? Revocation? Does it really matter? I can't fly anyway." She sighed and looked out the window. "Not with my panic attacks."

"It doesn't change anything," he said, taking her clammy hand. "In case you were worried that it would. It certainly doesn't change my feelings for you."

And what would those be?

Chapter 14

Ronan pulled up in front of her childhood home and put the car in park.

"This could be incredibly awkward," Cass said.

Ronan raised an eyebrow at her. "Meeting the parentals usually is."

She laughed. "That? No—well, there is that, I guess, but this is a whole other level of awkwardness. My stepfather, Jim, has been pressuring me to get back in the cockpit. Back on the horse, so to speak."

"Does he know?" Ronan asked, softly.

"About my panic?" She shook her head. "You're the only one who knows about that."

Despite his nervousness at meeting her family, the idea that she trusted him, that she'd shared what he figured was part of her ongoing psychological difficulty coping with the accident, sent warmth through his chest.

"Shall we go in and let the hostilities commence?" he asked, taking her hand.

"You okay?"

"Fine."

Ronan stood back as Cass greeted her mother, Tricia, in the entryway. He shook hands with the stepfather, Jim, a stocky, mustached man with a handshake like a vice, and then turned to Tricia, a neat, still-beautiful woman in her early sixties with the same worry lines across her forehead as Cass's, only deeper. Anderson appeared in his peripheral vision.

Cass gave her mother's shoulders a final squeeze and reached for Ronan, guiding him down the hall toward Anderson. He watched her gaze track the beer in Anderson's hand.

"Beer, Cass?" Jim asked.

Cass shook her head, and Ronan exchanged a look with Anderson, who looked as relieved as he felt. "Coffee," she said, "if you have it."

"We always have it, hon. Jim gave me one of those fancy pod machines for my birthday. I've got chai, flavored teas—"

"Plain black would be just fine," she interrupted.

"Ronan?" her mother turned to him with a smile.

"I'll get you a beer," Jim said, already heading into the kitchen.

"Great, thanks." Ronan forced a grin.

Cass followed Jim and Tricia into the kitchen, leaving him with Anderson in the hallway.

"She okay?" Anderson asked in a low tone.

"Yes, she's fine," he replied. She wouldn't thank him for discussing things with her father. Nevertheless, he couldn't help but feel sorry for the man. "How are you keeping?"

"Me?" Anderson took a step back and half a beat passed before understanding registered on his face. "Oh, yes. Her mother and I get along fine. We've had years to bury the hatchet—and it is buried—in a shallow grave." He smiled ruefully. "I'm just hoping it doesn't get unearthed today."

Ronan grunted.

"Is she … how's the … um."

"Drinking?"

The older man nodded.

"Not much."

Her father's shoulders sagged with relief. "I'm not saying she's an alcoholic or anything, just … it's never been bad before. Well, maybe in high school. I don't know. I wasn't around."

"She's finding other ways to cope," Ronan said smoothly.

Her father examined him, then cleared his throat. "Yes, well. Good. You're good for her."

Ronan took a swig of his beer. American crap. He put it on an end table.

"And you, Ronan? I can't tell you how impressed I've been with your team and your driving this season." Anderson gave him a hearty thump on the back. "Still on course to win it all."

"Yes."

Raised voices drifted in from the kitchen.

Anderson sighed. "That didn't take long, did it? Cass and Jim were always at loggerheads. I've heard the teenage years were a horror show."

"I'll go check on—"

"I'm coming with you."

Cass was standing with her back to him, her posture defensive.

Ronan went up behind her and put a hand on her shoulder. She glanced at him, her cheeks flushed, eyes narrowed with anger.

"Jim, I'm not going to keep telling you. Butt out!"

"Honey, all Jim is trying to say is that you need to get a new job, now, before you, before the … Jim lined something up with a tour operator in Vegas. The least you can do is go out there—"

"Mom, Jim, I'm not discussing this with you." This time when Ronan reached for her hand she clung to it. "I can't fly right now."

"But you have to," Jim insisted.

"She can't." Anderson said forcefully from the entryway.

All eyes turned to him.

"Stop harassing her about it. Jim, I understand your motivations, truly I do. But she's an adult and this is her decision."

"Anderson, this isn't any of your business. I know you mean well. And it's good that she was able to take a break, put the … incident behind her. But now she needs a job. You don't understand aviation. You don't know that if she waits until the report comes in, she won't have an opportunity—"

"Don't speak to my father that way," Cass said, her voice deceptively soft. "He's given me more than you could possibly understand these last few weeks."

Jim took a step back, his complexion a mottled red. "I'm trying to help you, Cass."

Cass straightened and pulled her hand from Ronan's grip. "I get that. But you can't."

"Cass, if you just—" Jim started.

"I can't fly!" she yelled.

There was dead silence.

"My God, Jim. You don't get it. You really don't get it. It's not like riding a horse, just get back on. I killed someone." She rubbed her forehead. "I killed someone," she repeated, dully.

Her mother choked on a sob.

"So your confidence is shaken," he said calmly.

She glanced at Ronan helplessly, shaking her head, her hands clenched into fists.

He met her gaze, his heart breaking for her. Should he step in here? She seemed to be holding her own, and this was her family.

Jim waved a hand in dismissal.

"Oh, honey." Her mother wrapped her arms around the taut figure of her child. But Cass held herself stiffly, not relaxing into the embrace.

Ronan's gaze moved to Jim. His face was set in stubborn lines. Cass had known he wouldn't accept this. And yet she'd still come here today. Subjected herself to this—his fierce disapproval, his persistence. Maybe this kind of attitude had worked on a troubled adolescent. But his pressure would never—and should never—work on an adult woman. Certainly not one like Cass who knew her own mind more than most people he'd ever met.

Anderson was half right. They were both stubborn achievers. That much was obvious. They set high standards for themselves and everyone around them, but that was where the similarities ended. Cass was idealistic, introspective, and sensitive beneath the confidence. And fully aware, now at any rate, that this accident would be something she'd always regret, always think about.

"I pulled strings to get you that interview and test flight next weekend."

"And I told you, repeatedly, not to do it." Her spine straightened, and she met her stepfather's glare with a calm expression, belied only by the hand squeezing the life from Ronan's again.

She turned to her mother. "Mom, Ronan and I can't stay."

Jim spun on his heel and left the kitchen through the garage door, slamming it on his way out.

"No, honey, please." Tears tracked down her mother's face. "Please stay. I'll talk to him."

"No."

She gave her mom a hug.

Anderson stood uncertainly in the doorway. "Should I?"

"Whatever you want." Cass said, reaching up to hug him. "I'll see you in Austin. Okay? And Dad?" She shot him a look of appreciation. "Thanks."

• • •

Her eyes were burning, but she would not cry. Ronan started the car without a word, and they'd made it four blocks before she managed to say, "I'm sorry, Ronan. That was ugly and embarrassing." Her throat so thick with tears she could barely speak.

He pulled the car to the curb in a move that made her throw a hand out to the dash to catch herself, put the car in park, and pulled her awkwardly across the console and into his warm body.

"Fuck," she choked out.

His hand gently stroked through her hair and down her back. She tried to tug away, but he didn't seem to want to let her go. Gradually one muscle after another in her face, her neck, her shoulders started to unclench in his warm embrace. He lifted her chin with a finger, wiped a few tears from her cheeks. "I'm in awe of you, you know."

She let out a watery giggle. "Then you're a lunatic."

"Back there? I wanted to throw something at your stepfather—possibly a punch, but equally likely my unfinished bottle of crap beer."

She laughed again, softly. "He has no frame of reference, and you can probably tell he's not big on the 'feels.'"

"Yes, that's one way of putting it, but good God, we were all telling him to back the hell off. And the old goat still persisted."

She sat back and gazed into his serious, hazel eyes. "He's clueless. And he's just not programmed to give that kind of emotional support to anyone. Not my mom and certainly not me. He loves me, but he wants me to move on, accept it."

"Feels mighty conditional to me—follow my advice or else. That's not the way paternal love is supposed to work, is it? Not that I'd know. It's a theoretical question."

That was the first time he'd brought up his father willingly, but it wasn't the time to bring another dysfunctional father into the conversation.

"I think Jim's just focused on fixing the problem, as if the problem is my career. When clearly it's a helluva lot deeper than that. It's been a rocky relationship, especially as I've gotten older and made choices he hasn't agreed with, but we've managed to maintain a basic level of respect—until now."

"Is he the main reason you became a pilot?"

"Only in the sense that he took me up with him on a flight and I fell in love with flying. Jim and I have struggled. I have to admit my two dads are quite a contrast."

"Yeah. Well, it's clear they both love you."

"Anderson has been one of two very bright spots," she gave Ronan a half smile, "in a pretty shitty year."

• • •

They were back in the hotel outside of Surprise, packing up before the meeting with EvacuAir, when Ronan decided to ask the question, to get it over with. "Are you going to see his widow?"

"I have to. But Mandy—she's not Steve. She's raising two kids by herself now, living with her parents in Dallas. She blames me for Steve's death. She's filed a lawsuit."

"Would it make you feel better to settle?"

"Settle?"

"Settle the lawsuit."

Her head cocked to one side and she considered him. "You know, that has occurred to me. I have assets. If it's just a matter of money …"

"I can give her the money."

She drew back. "Ronan, that's … that's very generous, but no, I can't let you do that."

"Cassidy, I'd do anything to help you work through this. And it would be easy. I have a trust set up. Most of the drivers who make the kind of money we do have something they put aside for charity. I donate to Doctors Without Borders, but some of the trust money goes to victims of my father's fraud—"

"Really?"

He drew her over to the loveseat and settled her in his lap, wrapping both arms around her. She leaned into his chest.

"You donate to your dad's victims?"

"Yeah. It's helped with some of the guilt I feel over Harry's crimes."

"Why would you feel guilty about what he did?"

"Because he might have gotten in to the degree that he did to help my career."

Her eyes narrowed and she shook her head. "From what Anderson tells me—"

He stiffened. She'd talked about his father with Anderson?

She squeezed the back of his neck. "Don't get all bent out of shape. Anderson told me about your dad and the trial. Your dad was committing fraud long before you came along. The guy managed to avoid criminal charges because his victims were embarrassed, but my dad knew someone who had dealings with Harry."

"Maybe. But the magnitude … well, it's at least partially because he wanted me to get to F1 and knew money was the way to do it. So shall I make a contribution or what?"

"No," she said, quickly. "But thank you for offering. It's something I need to take care of myself. Without your help, without Anderson's help. Without anybody's. But I appreciate it. More than you could ever know."

Stubborn, independent woman. Throwing money at his father's victims had gone a long way to assuaging his guilt. He could only hope the same might work for her. But something told him it wouldn't be as straightforward as that.

Chapter 15

Cass pointed to the small trailer-like building to the side of the runway at the tiny airport.

"Are you sure this is the place?" Ronan asked, his tone doubtful. Cass attempted a smile, which she was pretty sure fell flat. "No frills in aviation, Ronan. This is a totally different world than the one you inhabit."

She reached for the door handle, climbed out of the rented sedan, and grabbed her duffel with her gear.

There wasn't much. A few flight suits with the company logo, a jacket. Some manuals. Her night vision goggles and helmet had been repossessed at the hospital after the crash.

"This won't take long. I'll text you when I'm done," she said.

She'd only been to regional headquarters twice for training, but she remembered the cramped office near the small airport's hangars with white lettering indicating EvacuAir.

Ronan gave her a long look over his shoulder.

"There's a breakfast place in town I hear is good, but I doubt they have kippers or stewed tomatoes."

He smiled at her attempt at humor, but his eyes were worried. "Good luck."

She slammed the door wordlessly, slung the bag across her body like armor, and marched to the office door.

The office was bare bones. Like most things in aviation, it was all about function over aesthetics. She wouldn't be surprised if the corporate office in Georgia had this same utilitarian look, the same cheaply made furniture, with sheets of paper filled with regulations tacked onto the walls. The only decoration framed photos of a dozen helicopters and aviation pin ups.

A man in his mid-fifties with military bearing came through the door with a Styrofoam cup in his hand.

"Cassidy Miller?"

"Yep."

He switched the cup to his other hand and extended his arm. "Butch Villars, chief pilot for the region."

"What happened to Leon Summerfield?"

"Moved up to Georgia."

"Oh." Leon had been a known quantity at least. A stickler, but mostly fair.

"Why don't you come into my office?" He indicated a door to her right. She led the way and took a seat opposite a cluttered desk.

Instead of sitting behind the desk, he took the chair next to her. "I'm sure you know why you're here."

At her nod he continued. "We've completed our preliminary investigation. The FAA is still conducting theirs. We're letting you go."

No matter how much time she'd spent preparing for this moment, it still hit her like a blow, sucking all the air out of her body and leaving her dizzy and hollow with despair.

She nodded stiffly, focusing on her hands, twisting in her lap.

"I can imagine it feels pretty shitty—but before you go, I wanted to tell you a few things, off the record."

She looked up at his kind, sympathetic tone.

"I'm an old military pilot who hasn't been in the civilian world as long as you might expect. I saw a lot in my years of active duty service so I wanted to tell you not only what you did wrong, but what you did right."

"Thanks," she rubbed her forehead, "but that's not necessary. I know what I did. And I can't do it over the right way."

"Cassidy, you could be a pilot for a long time."

She stared, uncomprehending.

"You're a good pilot. You did as many things right as you did wrong. I've seen my share of bad weather and bad events, and nine times out of ten things just go to shit. I've been in that circumstance myself—you fly long enough, it can happen. Believe me, I understand the instinct to turn around and go back to where you came from. Our protocol—while still the safest thing to do—goes against instinct. And once you turned back, you probably could see again, yes?

She nodded.

"And then it got worse."

This was all in the report, but from the weary tone of his voice it sounded like he'd been there, done that.

"Putting down on mostly flat, isolated terrain at night—it wasn't a bad decision. Don't get me wrong—it wasn't the best decision you could have made. Following protocol would have been. But you did good landing her under those conditions. Unfortunately, the terrain didn't do you any favors."

Cass twisted her fingers in her lap.

"But—and this is the part I want you to take away, and why I think you're a good pilot who should stay in the profession—" That was the last thing she'd expected to hear. She held her breath as he continued.

"You shut her down as soon as your skids came down. That one action, that most critical thing, is something most pilots can't or don't do. With everything happening it gets overlooked, and without the shutoff, the risk of fire is damn near 100 percent."

She nodded. They'd been lucky.

"Two of three crew survived; that is the part you need to focus on. That and following the four C's in the future." He finished, looking at her, his expression expectant.

"I … I'm not sure I have a future," she said. "As a pilot, I mean."

"Then that would be a shame." He stood, indicating the interview was over. "There are some forms over there I need you to fill out. Your John Hancock and the date. They're marked with stickies."

"And the FAA?"

"You never know with the FAA; a suspension is possible. Revocation, unlikely."

She signed the documents he indicated.

"Thanks," she said.

"Best of luck," he responded.

She walked out into the sunlight, too dazed to call Ronan immediately. She spied an EvacuAir helicopter in the hanger, an Airbus AS350—an A Star, they called it. She crossed over the tarmac, into the hanger, and stared silently at the beautiful machine. She felt, rather than saw, Ronan's presence behind her.

Dashing away a few tears, she turned. He took two steps forward and caught her in his arms. Her breath escaped in a shuddering sob.

"That bad?" he asked, drawing back to look at her, concern making his eyes wide.

"It's hard to accept, even though I knew it was coming."

Butch had given her a degree of hope. A degree of understanding. And perhaps most important, hope that the FAA wouldn't take away her most important identity.

•••

"Cass, I won't be around much the next three days." The words drifted into her sleepy consciousness as she rolled over in the enormous bed. Everything in Austin, Texas, was oversized it seemed. The suite was gigantic. She urged her limbs into action and lifted her heavy eyelids. Ronan was toweling off his hair in the bedroom.

"What? I've been asleep." She glanced at her watch, "Three hours?" And you—you've been down at the gym again, haven't you?"

He raised his eyebrows and swiped up his jeans from the chair in the corner, eyeing her. She sat up fully. She'd slept in the middle of the day, and she'd been cold stone sober. That hadn't happened in a long time. "You make me feel like a sloth." Who knew racecar drivers were such health fanatics? Pilots most definitely aren't.

"Indeed," he said, as he dumped the pants back onto the chair. Even from across the room his intense gaze on her camisole-covered breasts sent a flood of desire through her.

He made his way purposefully across the room.

She straightened, pulling her hair over her shoulder and toying with the ends, on eye level with his swelling erection.

Any residual sleepiness cleared out, leaving the throb of desire and anticipation. What was it with Ronan? Whatever it was, her libido was perpetually in hyperdrive.

"Maybe you need some exercise now to atone for this laziness?" His hand rested on the top of her head.

She went to her knees, shoving sheets aside. Her hands grasped his hips, curling around the thick elastic of his boxer briefs. "Shall I begin atoning—this way?"

He drew in a breath.

She leaned forward and licked his rock-hard abdomen—his taste and smell barely apparent beneath the bath soap he'd just used. Pity. She liked the scent of him after a workout. All musky man. Her hands maneuvered his underwear down. He stepped out, his breath coming jerkily.

Cass raised her head, meeting hazel eyes slit with passion, and his hips bucked as her hand clasped his thick shaft.

"Cass," he said hoarsely.

Never breaking eye contact, she lowered her mouth, taking the fullness of his cock into her mouth inch by slow inch.

He shuddered, one hand gripping her shoulder, the other stroking the back of her head.

She pushed his legs apart, and he grunted, surging into her mouth.

Her mouth and tongue toyed with the tip and shaft of his cock as her fist worked the base.

"Cass," he growled. "Enough."

When she didn't stop, he moved his hips back, reaching into the drawer for a condom. "Okay, you're not listening, and I'm not arguing with you … definitely not …" His voice trailed off.

She flipped over onto all fours at the edge of the bed, shivering in anticipation and the chill in the room. Desperate. Impatient.

There was the sound of the condom being opened in the silence of the room, quickened breaths from him, and then he was there—his cock at her slick entrance.

She spread her legs wider, resting on her shoulder and face, barely able to see him behind her. He thrust, hard.

"Agh," she moaned.

He froze. "God, sorry—did I hurt you?"

She moved her hips against him in answer, seeking, desperate. "No, just—ah, don't stop."

"Sure?" he asked, in a strangled voice. And then he was driving into her, over and over. Her hand sought the swollen nub of her clit; she stroked herself and came hard, the mattress capturing her gasps.

His body stiffened behind her, and she watched from over her shoulder as his face contorted with ecstasy, the angles of his face sharply defined as he pulsed into her. Her hand found his balls high and tight against his body as he came, shouting her name.

He collapsed next to her on the bed and gave her an exhausted grin. "What the hell are you doing to me, woman?" Ronan hauled her up to his body; she curled against him.

What had he been saying before their needs obliterated conversation?

She pushed his shoulder playfully. "You mentioned something about three days?"

"Practice starts in a few days. We've signed up for the extra two-hour test session. Remember that tech I told you about? I think we're attempting it this race. Then debriefing, then press conference. Then sponsor function. And Saturday is—"

"Qualifier before Sunday. I know the deal." Cass flapped her hand at him. "While I lounge around here and live the life of leisure, you kill yourself with your fifteen-hour schedules."

He shrugged and trailed his finger down her side.

"Do you ever wonder whether it's worth it?"

He looked up sharply. "No."

"Your job really impacts your ability to have a life, doesn't it? Between the pre-race stuff and the promotion and sponsor events—"

He sat up, body half turned toward her, his mouth drawn into a determined line. "This is the life I want, the job I want. It isn't just about driving the bloody car around the track every Sunday." His tone was clipped. "I have to be there. I'm the one who'll be out there. I'm the one who'll go up in a blaze if I crash or go spinning off the track for whatever reason. Not the test driver, not the engineer, not the team coach. Me. No one else."

All playfulness had deserted him. No teasing. No sparkle in the eyes. Of course he was stressed this close to the end of his season. And something must've gone down at his meeting last night. He'd been more stressed than she'd ever seen him. And though he hadn't mentioned his father's release, it had to be weighing on him. And still he'd taken her up to Arizona for that disastrous family dinner and then the EvacuAir meeting. She swallowed her defensiveness and gripped his hand.

"Sorry. I'm keeping everything crossed for you. Listen, Anderson's picking me up for breakfast and I'll find stuff to do."

"Look, Cass—"

"No—it's okay, it's go time. I get it."

"It's not just that ... I ... I've been down this road before. The demands of the job. The demands of the relationship."

She held up both hands. "No, listen, that's not me. I'm not using the 'R' word. I'm concerned about you."

"Well I am using the 'R' word, and I know I'm a difficult person to be involved with. It's part of why my serious relationships have been few and far between. The job, the team, come first in my life."

Her stomach twisted. Well. That was blunt. And it hurt more than she'd expected. Not that she hadn't realized winning, his career were everything to him. And it wasn't like she was asking him to pledge his undying love or anything, but to be told in no uncertain terms where she stood in his life—it was off-putting.

He stood up again and moved about the room, tense as he gathered his watch, sunglasses, and phone-charging paraphernalia. He was jittery as all hell. Unreachable. It was always like watching a whole different person.

"I'm going to head to Dallas tomorrow. Mandy's living there with her parents; it's only three hours away."

He stared at her.

"Up and back. No big deal."

"Can you wait until after the race? I could go with you then."

"No, it's okay. I've decided to get it over with."

"Let me talk to my team. How many hours away? Up and back in a day?"

"Forget it, Ronan. You've got enough on your mind. I'll leave at noon and be back after dinner."

He blew out a breath. "That works then. I've got a meeting tomorrow morning. Can we leave at one?"

Cass toyed with the sheet. Did she want him to come? She couldn't ask Anderson. He didn't understand. And she was more terrified of Mandy than she'd been of the meeting with EvacuAir. But Ronan had so much going on.

He sat on the bed next to her and stilled her hand. "I'm coming with, Cass. We'll leave at noon."

She nodded, her throat thick with tears.

He kissed the top of her head and got up.

"Just two more races. That's it," he said, from the doorway.

She mustered a smile.

And then what? Lather, rinse, repeat next year and the year after? But she didn't dare ask.

Chapter 16

The three-hour ride to the Dallas suburbs on Wednesday was punctuated by little small talk. The closer it came to race day, the more strung out Ronan became. He hadn't been this stressed before any of the other races. It must be something to do with the end of the season and how close he was to winning it all. He'd been spending a lot of time with the engineers.

Her level of stress amplified as they approached Dallas. Guilt overwhelmed her. The mutual friend who had given her Mandy's new address had warned her that the woman was bitter. Apparently, Mandy was job hunting and needed her relatives to help with the kids. Cass's failure had totally uprooted their lives.

"Next right," she said tersely, slapping away the blue air freshener that he'd insisted on hanging from the mirror.

For once Ronan hadn't pulled his driving-too-fast stunt. Too bad. She was itching for an argument. Anything to diffuse some of the tension.

She looked down at the GPS on her phone, and then pointed to a large brick two-story home with an immaculately cared for lawn. "That one."

Ronan guided the car up to the curb in front.

"Cass?" he said gently, after a minute had passed and she'd made no effort to get out of the car.

"What has you so terrified? That she'll rage at you?"

"No. That she'll be broken. That the kids … I don't know. But my gut is telling me to get the hell out of here."

"I thought you didn't believe in all that gut feeling stuff," he teased.

She ignored it. "I don't even know what I'm going to say."

"If your gut is telling you not to do it … best not."

"I have to." She grasped the door handle and was out of the car before she could reconsider. There were two cars in the driveway: Steve's old red, dented crew-cab Ford pickup, and Mandy's new silver Mazda. The in-law vehicles were nowhere in sight.

Steve and Mandy were one of those couples whose vehicles said a lot about who they were. Mandy was a good mother, a good wife, a good dental hygienist, and a genuinely nice person, but she practically screamed high maintenance with her long, platinum locks, her skinny jeans, knee-high boots, and midriff-baring tops. Not that Steve had talked about her much, but when he had, it'd been with a kind of reverence.

She'd been so lost in thought, she hadn't noticed Ronan had exited the vehicle.

"Ronan. I'm not doing this with you."

"Oh yes you are. The work thing, I get that you had to do alone, but not this."

She relented. She needed whatever support she could get.

"At least the kids won't be home," she said as she approached the door.

They climbed the steps. Cass's finger was poised above the doorbell when she heard the unmistakable shriek of a child.

"Shit." She backed away. It was one in the afternoon. What the hell were the kids doing home?

The brown door flew open. In the entryway stood Mandy, harried, disheveled, and enraged if the look on her face was anything to go by. Very far from the picture of sleek perfection Cass remembered. Her youngest son was on her hip. A son who looked just like Steve.

Cass felt Ronan's comforting presence behind her.

"What the fuck?" Mandy said, ignoring her son's presence. "My lawyer told me you might try this. I told him you didn't have the guts."

Cass backed up another step, into Ronan's body.

He steadied her with his hands.

"He told me not to say anything to you, but I've got a few things to get off my chest."

Cass chewed her lip, looking at the red-eyed, tow-headed kid on her hip. "I'm sorry if this is a bad time."

"It's all a bad time now, Cassidy. Every fucking day is bad. Steve is dead." The child's eyes were huge now. She needed to leave. If only to prevent the little boy from hearing all of this.

"I'm so sorry. I wanted to let you know … I … how sorry I am. If there's anything I can do …"

"Really? An apology?" She emitted a sharp crack of humorless sound that could've been a laugh.

Cass flinched, and the child started to cry, burying his face in his mother's neck.

"You are something else," the woman said wearily, holding her son to her body. "Just get out. You won't find anything here."

"If there's anything I can do …"

"Cassidy, I had to move back home with my parents. My parents. Our Arizona house is a short sale. I can't keep up with the payments, and God only knows when EvacuAir's insurance policy will come through. I lost my job because someone needs to take care of these kids and Steve's not around to help me."

"I'll do whatever I can. I'd be happy to give you—"

Mandy's mouth curled. "You won't give me anything. But I'll take everything I can from you. Everything. And it still won't matter." Her eyes filled with tears. "Because you took the only thing that mattered from me. Now get the fuck off our property before I call the police."

The boy looked up at her words, shocked but eager, searching the street.

Mandy slammed the door.

Ronan tried to put an arm around her, but she shrugged it off. "Please, just … just leave me alone."

The tears started before they'd even reached the car—once inside, she pressed a shaking fist to her mouth to contain the sobs.

"Cass," he started.

"Just … don't. I can't—" her voice broke as all the guilt and self-loathing rushed up to choke her. She'd give anything to be alone right now. Anything. Instead, she had a three-hour ride back to Austin, with the only break a stop for gas and food. On their way out of town, Cass swiped at the tears tracking down her face and pointed to a liquor store next to a gas station. "Stop there."

He cast a final, worried glance her way before getting out of the car. She, too, climbed out and headed for the liquor store while he put gas into the tank. As she paid for the bottle of bourbon, she watched him walk into the food mart.

Cass waited on the sidewalk outside the convenience store, continuing to track his movements through the glass door as he grabbed a few sodas and waters, along with a couple of snacks for the ride. He lifted a bag of chips and she nodded. Whatever. It wasn't like she could eat anything.

They settled back into the car for the long ride home. Dusk came and went and she drank steadily from the liquor bottle—escaping the car, Ronan, and her guilt.

She leaned her head against the doorjamb and stared out at the endless flat scrub of Texas.

•••

Ronan was still an hour from Austin when his passenger slumped in her seat. He hadn't said a word for the last two hours as she took pull after pull from the bottle before finally recapping it and tossing it, half-empty into the floorboard. Up until that disastrous meeting with the widow, she'd been coming to terms with everything mostly without drinking. After that scene, though, he could understand why Cass turned to the pain-numbing comforts of alcohol. Hell, he probably would, too. That woman,—she'd been desperate, stricken.

Twenty-miles later, Cass was still unconscious and emanating alcohol fumes when blue and white lights lit up in the rearview mirror.

Bugger.

He eased off the accelerator, braked, and pulled over to the shoulder. He put the car in park and waited, heart pounding. He didn't have a U.S. license—he had one from the U.K.—and God knows with his lead foot he'd been pulled over in plenty of countries. Most places around the globe he'd just offer up a few large bills and go on his way. Not in America, and not at home. Those were two places one did not give bribes. At least that's what he'd heard. He hadn't had the misfortune of being caught out in either of those two places.

Cass mumbled something and sat up.

"Go back to sleep," he said, tersely, watching the uniformed officer approach in the rearview mirror.

"Why are we stopped?" she slurred. "Where's my drink?"

"You finished it." He powered his window down with the button. "Seriously, Cass, I'm being pulled over for speeding, so it's best if you just go back to sleep, or just pretend to sleep."

She frowned, sweeping the tangled mass of hair from her eyes. "I told you, you drive too fast."

"License and registration?"

"Certainly, officer." He leaned across Cass to find the registration easily in the rental car glove compartment. He lifted the paper and handed it to the young officer.

Then he dug around in his back pocket while the officer lit up the car with his flashlight beam. Cass cringed and put up a hand. The light swept the vehicle, stopping on the half-empty bottle of Makers Mark on the floorboard.

"I'm going to need you to step out of the vehicle, sir."

Goddamn it.

The cop was examining his license. "You from England?"

"Yes, sir."

"Can you drive here with this thing?" he asked giving the license a shake.

"I assume so; I'm driving this Saturday."

Cassidy leaned over him. "He's driving a Formula One car for Pan—" She hiccupped. "Pantech."

He gave her a gentle push back into her seat.

"Hey!" She pushed him back. "Don't do that."

"Mr. Hawes, I need you to step out of the vehicle."

"Stay put." Ronan said, warningly.

She folded her arms across her chest and glared at both men.

"Have you been drinking this evening, sir?"

"No."

"Sir, it smells of alcohol in the vehicle, and there's a half-empty bottle of liquor."

"Yes, my—er—" This was no time to have an existential crisis about what she was to him. "My girlfriend got some bad news today, and she had the bourbon—well, most of it."

The man leaned toward him slightly, nostrils flaring. "It's illegal in this state to have an open container of alcohol in a moving vehicle, sir. And grounds for a sobriety test."

"I understand."

"Come with me to the rear of the vehicle, please."

Up close the stocky chap was barely more than a kid—early twenties, lean, unlined face. And clearly nervous. Ronan sighed inwardly. The rookies were always by the book.

"Do you know the speed limit on this stretch of road, sir?" The man asked.

"Uh ... no, actually." Yes, he'd been lost in thought, but considering he thought of speed signs as a suggestion for lesser drivers, Ronan never paid them much heed. And he was used to thinking in kilometers anyway. "No, no, I don't."

"Well, it's seventy. And my radar indicated you were going eighty-eight."

He acknowledged this with a grim nod.

"Sir, do you have any injuries that would prevent you from doing this testing or cause you problems? Problems with your back, legs, knees—"

"No. Let's get on with this." Ronan crossed his arms across his chest.

"Do you have balance issues, middle ear trouble, vertigo—"

Ronan sighed. Yep, by they book. If only they saw the tests his body had been put through as a driver for reflexes, balance, and flexibility. "No."

The man checked a few boxes on his pad. "Now I need you to stand with your feet together, arms at your side."

Ronan complied.

The sound of a car door opening prompted the officer to move around to the passenger side of the rental car.

"Ronan?" Cass said.

"Ma'am? I need you to get back in the car."

"I have to pee," came Cass's plaintive tones. "Officer."

"You'll have to wait."

"No," she insisted. "I can't."

"Cass," Ronan said in his most authoritative tone. "Get back in the car. Let me finish up here and we'll deal with that."

"Ma'am, back in the vehicle."

"Maybe you should just let her pee," Ronan suggested with what he hoped was a conspiratorial smile.

The man scowled. "If she doesn't get back in the car, I'll cuff her and put her in mine."

"Then you might have a very wet car seat," he suggested, half tempted to let him try it.

Cass staggered into the underbrush, and the officer cursed. He pulled the radio from his belt and called for backup.

•••

Thirty minutes later they were handcuffed in the back of the police car en route to the station. Cass had been—there was no other word for it—belligerent. She hadn't turned physical but she'd been waving her arms, interfering with the sobriety test they had been attempting to give him. The officer had finally lost patience, and who could blame him?

"Cass," he said, as they put the handcuffs on him, "just go along with this, okay? Quietly."

When they did the same to her she muttered, "Oh my God. Oh my God." She thumped her head against the vinyl seatback, over and over.

"Calm down." Could she have a panic attack drunk? Maybe he should say something before the officer whipped out his baton or taser. "Just cooperate, okay? I'll contact a friend—"

"I need to call Anderson."

"Okay." He spoke, calmly. "Cass, we'll be separated when we get there. They'll test me, I imagine. Just please, do what they say."

She looked over at him, eyes bloodshot. "I'm sorry, Ronan. Now I'm fucking up your life, too."

"It's okay, Cass. It's all going to work out."

She shook her head and the despair in her eyes gave him a hollow feeling in his chest.

The ride to the police station didn't take long. It was a small town—Henderson according to the signs. There wouldn't be much chance of a photographer or reporter who just happened to be around. The older officer brought him in the two-story building, the American and Texas flags out front the only signs that it was a municipal building.

He waited on a bench, still cuffed, for someone, probably the supervisor.

A tall, swarthy man wearing a white shirt arrived. He was about fifty and had the look of someone who'd seen and done it all.

"Evenin', son."

"Officer."

"You a Brit?"

"Yes, sir."

"What you doing speeding through my county?"

"Occupational hazard, sir. I'm a racecar driver."

The man studied him a minute. "In town for the race in Austin?"

"Yessir."

"Huh. Might be I know a little something about that race." He stared at Ronan a moment more, then turned on his heel, calling for the sergeant. The sergeant, the man who had brought him in apparently, appeared from an office down the hall.

"Get the breathalyzer. Test him."

"Okay, captain."

A few minutes later Ronan finished blowing into the device.

"I'll go tell the captain you're clean."

The older man appeared in the doorway. "Nothing?"

"No sir, zeros straight across the board."

"I made a few calls. We'll get the paperwork going and release you."

"And my companion?"

"Her, too."

"And our car?"

"Hasn't been impounded yet. I arranged for a ride for you back to your vehicle."

They led Ronan to the building lobby. He sat, waiting. Ten minutes passed before a subdued Cass joined him.

"God, I'm so sorry, Ronan. So sorry," she whispered.

He strove for anger, but all he ended up with was pity. She looked so wrecked, pale and fragile with glassy eyes. "You feeling sick?"

She nodded.

He cradled her back in his arm and she leaned into him, her silent tears leaking into his shirt. Tenderness welled up. "I know, Cass. And I get what you've been through. I've seen how awful this is for you. How unfair. How gut wrenching. But drinking is making it worse. You have to figure out something other than alcohol to help you cope."

"I know, I thought I had a handle on it, I thought I was getting better, and then …"

"Cass, the thing is, with something like this, you're going to have good days and bad days—for a while would be my guess. And you can't just drink to cope with the bad. Talk to someone, a professional. Anyone who can help with what you're going through. Do you think I haven't noticed your nightmares? The insomnia? I've seen you do incredibly brave things this week. Don't think I don't know what it cost you or how much I admire you. It's just … the drinking. I can't …"

"It scares me, too."

They both looked up as the exit door opened, and the last person in the world he wanted or expected to see walked through.

Ronan was tempted to call a cab, ask a cop—anything but take a ride from Maddux. But at 1:00 A.M., in a tiny Texas town, and Cass's complexion gray with a combination of hangover and remorse, he'd force himself to accept the offer. The effort of trampling down the walls of his pride brought him out in a cold sweat. "What the hell are you doing here?" Ronan asked.

"I grew up one town over. The deputy who picked you up is a high school buddy, so he called me once he realized who you were. I offered to come help you out, you and Cassidy. Hey, Cass." He grinned, that good-ole-boy, aw-shucks grin.

Cass, to her credit, completely ignored him.

Ronan clenched his fists. That grin in particular begged to be wiped off his face.

"Where's the car?" Maddux asked, tossing his keys repeatedly. The man was like a hyperactive child. All nervous fits of energy.

"Route 43."

Ronan took Cass's clammy hand and led her into the unseasonably cold night.

Maddux stopped in front of a black Mustang Cobra.

Ronan eyed it. "This your car?" American muscle car. Figured.

"Yep," The other man's drawl seemed much more pronounced here—and more grating.

Maddux unlocked the car, and Ronan brushed him out of the way to open the door for her.

The other man grinned.

"Ronan, I am so sorry—" Cass whispered.

"Not to worry, love," he brushed a kiss on the top of her head as she ducked to climb in. He shut the door behind her.

"That was fast," Maddux said, nodding at Cass through the window.

"What was?" Ronan stopped in his path to the passenger front door to make eye contact with Maddux over the hood.

"Nautilus Oil?" he said. "Not bad, man. I wish I'd thought of it. Tap that, get Daddy on board."

"Excuse me?" Ronan's eyes narrowed, his hand froze reaching for the door handle.

"Miller's daughter, yeah?"

Was the man implying that Ronan would sleep his way into a sponsorship? It was all he could do not to laugh.

"And Nautilus has had it with Simons. Wish I'd thought of that. Looks like I did you a solid taking Vivienne off your hands." Maddux opened his door with more force was strictly necessary.

"Maddux?"

"Yeah?" The man settled into the driver's seat and shut the door. "Shut the fuck up, will ya?"

Unoffended, the mad man grinned and fired up the V8 engine. He glanced over his shoulder. "Cass, all right?"

She didn't say anything, leaned her head back on the seat, and closed her eyes. Ronan could've sworn he saw a tear tracking down her cheek, reflected in the light.

• • •

Cass climbed out of the rental car at the hotel lobby while Ronan went to park. She made her way, still drunk and slightly unsteady to the front desk.

"One room, three nights, please," she said, handing her credit card to the reception clerk behind the counter. It was late. Very late, and Ronan had testing tomorrow at the track. Now wasn't the time to have it out with him about what she'd overheard. The room wasn't spinning, but her stomach was heaving. Could what Maddux said be true? Was Ronan's team eyeing a Nautilus sponsorship? And Anderson had said he wished Ronan were wearing his logo. The man handed her a slip to sign, then gave her a room key in an envelope.

She wouldn't believe it of him. After his performance this season, he could attract any sponsor this close to the championship. On track to win it all.

But when she'd met Ronan, his team hadn't been doing so well. He'd been plagued by engine troubles in the first half of the season.

Of course Nautilus wanted to team up with a winner. Its pockets were more than deep. And the owners had a hard-on for the sport. Always had. They'd been in F1 since its inception.

Ronan met her at the elevator.

"Cass, you all right?"

She managed what she hoped was a smile in his direction. She was sick and exhausted. And sick of being sick and exhausted. Maybe the time spent cuffed at the police station was her wake-up call. She hadn't been put in a cell, but it might have come to that.

She put up a hand to cover her burning eyes.

He rubbed his hand down her back, and it was all she could do not to flinch.

"What is it?"

"How can you even ask me that?" she said.

God, he'd been through a lot of trouble on her behalf. For something that had started out casual, things sure had sped up in a hurry. And him just out of a relationship. Maybe there was something to this sponsorship thing.

The elevator doors opened. She got in, checked the room number on the envelope and pushed her floor button. Then his.

She could feel him staring at her.

"What's going on here?" he said.

"I got my own room."

The doors opened, and she stepped into the hallway. He followed her out. She turned and put up a hand. "Don't. Just don't."

"Are you angry with *me*?"

"Is there any truth to it?"

"To what?" His expression was genuinely baffled.

"To the sponsorship thing. Anderson."

"What? Did you hear that?" He took a step back. "Just Maddux talking out of his arse again. That's way up the food chain. Naught to do with me."

"It sure would make your life easier though, wouldn't it? Pantech has been on the rocks financially."

"That could be said of any number of sponsors this season, in this economy."

"Let me put it plainly then. Are you with me," the words caught in her throat, "because of Nautilus?"

A flush rose up, darkening his jawline, his cheekbones. His expression contorted into anger—no, rage. She'd never seen that particular look on his face, and she backed up a step.

"After everything?" He turned and punched the button for the elevator. "How could you even ask me that?" The elevator was still there and the doors opened. He stepped inside, pushed his floor button and turned to look at her. His expression of hurt, pain mixed with anger, took her breath away. He never lost eye contact with her as the doors closed.

She put a hand to her mouth. Oh dear God. She was cracking up. Officially losing it. She pulled out her plastic room key and stumbled down the hallway to her room.

Chapter 17

Cass pushed two fingers against a throbbing temple. She'd had a headache for a day and a half thanks to that bout of drinking. It had been the hangover from hell, and she'd begged off all Anderson's invites. The sun and the roar of the cars weren't doing her any favors. She was still rehydrating. Depression had settled in, and even watching Ronan race didn't muster up enthusiasm. It mustered dread.

"Anderson?"

"Yes?"

"Is Nautilus looking to sponsor Ronan's team?"

"Unlikely."

"Why?"

"If they win, it's a boon to Pantech globally. Despite the setbacks the company has had this year, I don't see it dumping the team. Pantech is new to F1, but they've had great success—its engineering team is genius. And Nautilus isn't looking to be a secondary sponsor. We want our name front and center. So the short answer is no, not as things stand. But it's been a consideration."

So there was something to it.

"Does Ronan know?"

Anderson looked surprised. "I'm sure he's been in meetings where it's been discussed. Alternative sponsorships and the like, given the last two dismal years Pantech had financially. Why?"

"I just ... I didn't realize it was in the works."

"It isn't. Are you thinking this has something to do with you?" he said, gently.

She nodded.

"I don't think that's the kind of man Ronan Hawes is. He's many things, Cass. Single-minded, certainly arrogant. But he's not calculating. I'm a pretty good judge of character, hon."

"Yes. So am I," she said quietly. She pretended to turn her attention back to the track.

"That can't be right." Anderson checked the stopwatch and gave it a brisk shake.

"What?" she said.

"Nothing."

"I can see by your expression it's not nothing, Anderson." Cassidy turned back, her binoculars trained on Ronan's car as he did his victory lap after the preliminary race for starting position.

"He's faster than anyone out of the turns. That lap time was phenomenal," her father finally admitted, raising his own binoculars.

"Too fast?" she said. "No such thing. If he wins tomorrow, he'll be within a point of Maddux going into the final race. I think he said something about new tech they're trying out."

Her father's gaze swung to her. "New tech?"

Crap. She shouldn't have said anything. Top secret probably.

"Never mind."

"What new tech?" Anderson pressed.

"Dad. You're asking me?"

"I heard they were developing something preseason. But it flamed out, literally, in testing."

"What?"

"Burned up a car. It was fast, some kind of legal traction control. It was all very hush-hush. I thought they stopped development on it after the incident."

"What incident? Dad, you're scaring me."

"We're probably not talking about the same thing, Cass."

"There was an incident?" she pressed.

"They had some new legal system of traction control, something that bypassed all the regulations against it; at least that was the rumor. They were on the accelerator faster than anyone else out of the turns, setting track records last winter in preseason testing. And then there was a fire. No one was seriously injured."

Cassidy fought to keep her nerves under control and turned to look at him.

"Shall we go down and congratulate him?" her father asked with what she recognized to be feigned heartiness.

Cass pulled him down into the chair next to her.

"I'm a little freaked." She tightened her grip on his arm.

Anderson looked away.

Cass's eyes narrowed. "You think they're using this thing, whatever it is, in his car, don't you?"

Anderson toyed with his stopwatch. "His times have dropped today. End of season, this close, there's a lot at stake." He shrugged.

Horror flooded her brain, but she fought to keep her voice clam. "This change could be dangerous."

"If they're using it, they've worked out the problems."

"I need to talk to him about it." She rose from her chair.

Anderson grabbed her wrist. "Cass, you can't just go charging up—"

"Why not?"

"Because it's not—he won't … he won't be receptive to your concerns."

"And if they haven't? Worked out the issues? "

"That's what I think you don't understand, Cass. That you've never understood. These guys are willing to die or risk serious injury to win a race. They strap themselves into an engine that careens at two hundred plus miles per hour around circuits made just for these cars and around city streets all over the world. They're not just competitive, they are the most competitive bastards on the face of this earth."

Cass stared at him, open-mouthed.

He shook his head. "Ronan's not a bad guy. He's earned my respect with the way he cares for you, but you're not going to change who he is."

"Someone willing to burn up in a car for the chance to win a race?"

Her father sighed. "Cass, every last one of those guys will do anything to win. It's part of what makes them great—driver, engineer, crew—the whole lot of them. This is the pinnacle of vehicle engineering. That race. The car. And you, my dear, are an idealist if you imagine otherwise."

"I can't believe you would condone something like that."

"I've seen this sport through most of its incarnations. The engineering, the money, the fame. You've only seen a hint of it because you're American, but people worship these guys—they are larger than life. When they win, the nationalism, it's—you've never seen anything like it. The World Cup is the only thing that comes close. Your American sports events can't touch this sport for worldwide appeal."

"So that makes it okay?"

"I didn't say that. But these people know what they are walking into with F1. From the driver on down. Traveling with a vehicle seven months of the year is like a circus: pull down, tear down, travel hundreds or thousands of miles, repeat, over and over. All for the chance to be the best in the world—or contribute to the team that makes that happen. It's so much more than just a car race; it's a feat of engineering. If you're not at the top of your game in your capacity, you've no place in F1. You'll be chewed up and spit out. These decisions about the vehicles are made by owners, by Pantech-Windsor. The driver—he's the icing, not the cake."

He was beginning to sound remarkably like Ronan. Or rather, like how Ronan had spoken to her when they'd first met. "What if it isn't safe? "

"These vehicles have all the safety bells and whistles. They don't want to kill a driver or wreck a car, But fortune favors the bold."

"And if it's not legal, this new, faster, more dangerous technology?"

"They'll be penalized."

"Permanently?"

"Nothing is permanent in this sport."

"Death is," she said bitterly, slumping back in her seat.

•••

At the press event after the prelims, Cass spied Ronan before he saw her. She eased farther back into her alcove, watching him glide through the excited crowd, scoping out the scene with hawk-like vision. His body language said "tense"—as tense as she was feeling. His progress was hindered by shoulder pats, excited female squeals of joy, air kisses, and real smooches. Someone even tried to plant a Texan cowboy hat on him, but he smoothly wriggled away from his clusters of admirers. There must be some other explanation for his times. She couldn't believe he'd risk his life and the life of the other drivers for some potentially dangerous new technology.

She caught his eye.

His step faltered.

"You did fantastic—really quick."

"Thanks." His expression was distant. "Well ..." He indicated the people waiting to talk to him.

"No, go ahead," she said, her heart aching in her chest. So this is how it would end. In a hallway, after a race, because of a drunken, unforgivable accusation. If she could just talk to him. Explain. But with the race tomorrow and whatever was going on with the car, he didn't need the distraction.

Ronan had taken two steps down the hall away from her when Anderson broke away from the group he was talking to, turned around, and shook Ronan's hand. "Well done." He looked at him quizzically. "You certainly pulled it all together in last four laps."

"Thanks, Mr. Miller, but as you know, it all comes down to tomorrow."

Cass turned from her father and almost collided with another tall man. She looked up into the Maddux's sculpted face, his green eyes glittering with some unidentifiable passion. Whatever it was, it was directed at Ronan. "Nice to see you again, Mr. Hawes," he drawled, mimicking Ronan's accent, badly. His arched eyebrows lifted as he turned to her, allowing his gaze to wander from her forehead to her chest and back up again. Without a doubt, she was being mentally undressed. "And you, Ms. Miller—looking quite … sober today."

"Screw you," she replied.

Maddux grinned and raised his glass of neon orange Supernova in the direction of the bar. There she was, Vivienne McCloud. Flirting with a group of men in Supernova Energy gear. "And there's Viv. Socializing as usual," he grinned.

Ronan didn't respond and didn't look up.

"You seem mighty worked up, Hawes," Maddux said, clasping him on the shoulder. "I suppose you're thinking, so near and yet so far."

"You've no idea what I'm thinking," Ronan said, knocking off Maddux's arm.

"Here's what *I* was thinking." Maddux lashed on the Texan accent now. "I was thinking you were damn fast out there today. I sure don't know how you did it getting out of the turns so quickly."

Ronan took a long swig of his drink.

Maddux never moved his hooded eyes from Ronan's face. "Or maybe I do know but don't wanna."

"Go to hell, Maddux. Just take care not to take anyone along with you."

Maddux exhaled, eyes narrowing. "I could say the same. You better be pretty damn sure whatever you've got going on won't endanger us all, y'hear?"

• • •

Less than twenty-four hours later, Ronan yanked off his helmet after the race and took two steps toward his smiling engineer, Benny.

"What in the bloody hell is going on? Is this damned machine ready or not?"

The other man's smile slid off. "You won, didn't you?"

Jaw clenched, stiff with fury, Ronan grasped the man's elbow, his fire retardant gloves starkly white against the crimson jumpsuit. He dragged him a few feet from the rest of the crew who were watching silently. "Yeah, but I don't fancy burning up to do it. It's hot in there." He gestured to the car. "The engine temp was up, way up."

"We're so close, mate. So close. Only Hockenheim—"

"The hell man, this is the same problem we had preseason, before the fire. I had same indicators flashing at me that I did in the test runs, the same warning signs Gregor had before the fire. I was told the issues had been resolved."

"They're still toying with it. Setting parameters—"

"Toying with it. Toying with it?" His voice rose an octave. "This is my life here, man. And the lives of the other drivers. Either it's ready—as in fail-safe—or it isn't. So which is it?"

"It's bloody well genius, that's what it is, and you know it. You were out of the turns faster than anyone else—"

"Yeah, just like Silverstone. Until the bloody thing blew, and Gregor barely escaped the car! Jesus, Benny."

"One more race. We need this."

Ronan put a gloved hand to his forehead.

"I've seen the weather for Germany next week." Benny said. "It'll be a monsoon, and you know how Maddux does in the wet. I wouldn't want to be on the racetrack with him, and it's just one more win at stake, mate."

Ronan was already shaking his head. "No."

"It's not your decision, is it?"

He took two steps from his engineer. "It has to be all there or nothing. No half measures in this sport."

The other man shrugged. "Comes with the job. If you were to ask any man there," he nodded in the direction of the drivers and crew gathering post-race, "do you know what they'd say? They all want to win. They would use the tech, ready or not."

"Is it ready?"

Benny raised his eyebrows. "Ready enough for you to win today."

Ronan tugged at his collar, his hair matted with sweat despite the cool temperatures in Austin.

The man reached out a hand, his expression placating. "Don't go off halfcocked."

Ronan gave him a final glare and strode toward the podium, helmet in hand.

• • •

Cass slumped in her padded seat, and Anderson leaned down with concern in his expressive blue eyes.

"You okay?"

She nodded. Spent. The excitement she'd felt watching him race in Brussels and Abu Dhabi was gone; terror had taken its place. She'd been frantic with worry and tension for the past hour. Now that he'd won, all the stress had dissipated, leaving her limp and chilled in the skybox. Cass's gaze searched and held on Ronan smiling up there on the podium. Her attention then wandered to Maddux, and she couldn't help but chuckle as Ronan directed the spurting bottle of champagne directly at him. The American's smile slipped—for a split second she almost felt sorry for the man. It was obvious that second place was good for nothing to him.

Anderson settled himself next to her. "Upset?"

"We had a fight. I think it's over. Which is ironic, considering I just hung up on a reporter who wanted to ask a few questions about being in police custody with Ronan. They're going to harass me until they get their story."

"It's a shame the press has run with it, but it's all speculation, and the town sheriff is telling everyone it was a misunderstanding. It will blow over; don't worry. "

Cass sighed. "How bad will I make things for him?"

"His reputation is unassailable overseas. Now it is at any rate. And everyone loves a winner. Sure, the American press will latch onto it, but Europeans aren't Texas fans, as you well know. They think Texans are the very devil incarnate."

Cass raised her brows. "Yeah?"

"Oh yes. If anything, the PR machine will play it up and Ronan will come out of this unscathed—. the 'victim' of the American media and the Texas good old cowboy culture. They know just how to spin it."

"Doesn't make it any less humiliating or less painful," she said in an under voice, staring out at the tarmac track blindly. She'd doubted Ronan's integrity on the sponsorship thing, despite everything they had, and all because of her insecurities. How dumb could she be?

As far as the new technology in his car went, he wouldn't race if it hadn't checked it out. She was worrying for nothing, just adding to the litany of stupid things she'd done since she'd met him. Ronan wasn't the kind of man to drive a car that could incinerate him and endanger all the other drivers. Good for him that his engineers had given him an eleventh hour shot. The crew at Silverstone had probably been working around the clock to have it ready for the end of the season.

• • •

He'd get nowhere with Pantech's boss, Martin, that much was certain.

There was a sponsor event—a celebration he was supposed to be headed for—but Ronan couldn't bring himself to dress for it. Instead, here he sat in the white hotel robe on the sofa, staring at his hands.

He wanted to win.

Was that so wrong? After so many years as runner-up, this was still his year. He didn't need the new technology to win. All he and Mitchell needed were a few points in Hockenheim.

There was a knock on the door, and he groaned, fitting his head into his palms.

Cass?

He opened the door to Martin Spruce, Pantech boss.

The man glanced down the hall, then pushed his way in. Ronan stepped back.

"As you can see," he gestured to his robe, "I'm not prepared for visitors."

Spruce crossed his arms. "This won't take long."

Ronan straightened.

"I understand you aren't happy with the hybrid technology we've put in the car."

"I'm happy about the speed and the control; I'm less pleased by the idea that all the kinks haven't been worked out and it's prone to ignite."

"You've one more race, Ronan. One more to win it all for us." The other man's eyes blazed with intensity. "We deserve this. This sport isn't just about one man—or any one man's fears. Your job is to drive."

"Yes. Let's talk about our jobs. My job is to drive my Formula One car to the outside edge of its limits. Your job is to provide me with a car that meets the safety parameters, rules, and guidelines set by our racing authority. Our job is to determine if the new technology is ready for prime time or to go back to the drawing board. My experience in the car at the end of the race indicates there are still problems with the new system. Significant problems. If it isn't ready, I don't race with it."

The other man snorted. "I don't have a single person on this crew—no, on this *team*—who doesn't want to win it all. You drivers." He shook his head. "The arrogance."

"This isn't a test track, Martin. I'm not the only one racing out there. Get it together without the danger of incineration, and we can keep it. I don't shy away from modifications. And I want to win, too. Have you forgotten what happened to Gregor at Silverstone? I can assure you, I haven't."

"What aspect of any of this business is safe? You want safe, be a bloody chartered accountant. I pick these people, from the engineers to the mechanics to the back office people, because they're exceptional—people who will accept nothing less than success, who'll go the extra mile. No matter the risk."

Martin took two steps toward the door. "We've come this far. I'm not going to let your fears jack it up," he warned. "We'll do whatever's necessary to win at Hockenheim. Now get dressed and get downstairs and play your part." He opened the door, checked the hallway, and was gone. The door snicked closed.

One more race.

One more.

Ronan sagged against the wall. He needed sleep. Once the adrenaline fled his system, he was punchy—exhausted and disgusted. And goddamn it all, heartbroken.

* * *

Cass checked her phone. No texts from Ronan. No voicemail. No contact. Not that she'd expected it. Yesterday after the prelims, she'd left a voicemail apology, told him she'd like to talk before he left Texas, and wished him well in the race. Now that he'd won, she wasn't above stalking him.

Anderson was right. Either Ronan was an ethical person or he wasn't. He was. Her gut was telling her he was.

True to her prediction, the press situation was a nightmare, and the guilt was overwhelming. They'd spotted her in the hotel lobby returning from the track after Ronan's win, and they'd followed her to her room, shouting questions at her. She'd been holed up here for the past three hours, and had to call down to the front desk when a reporter claiming to be room service had knocked repeatedly on her door. Only the memory of what her last bout of drinking had done was keeping her from the minibar. She'd have to leave at some point. There was only so much bad television she could stand. The news came on at 6:00 P.M., and she watched with a kind of horrified fascination as they'd discussed the outcome of the race and the alleged "arrest," hinting some kind of cover up and suggesting Ronan had been intoxicated, too.

There was still a part of her that couldn't understand why he stuck around. Why he put up with her drinking, her nightmares, her fucking panic attack. Here was a guy who had a complicated job, a life of endless travel and tremendous pressure, yet he'd taken her on, with all her issues. And now look what was happening—because of her.

Last night she'd had more nightmares. Thank God Ronan hadn't been around to witness them. She'd spent most of the night afraid to fall back asleep—reliving the crash in endless vivid loops, unwilling to escape with her old friend booze, which seemed to be causing more trouble than it solved. And she had to apologize to Ronan. If the press was causing her this much trouble, she could only imagine how they were hounding him. God. She'd track him down one way or another and make him listen to her apology.

• • •

Ronan dressed for the after-party. He still had a part to play until he could figure out how to proceed. What right *did* he have to decide risk? These were decisions Pantech-Windsor made—well above his pay grade. The whole damn thing was risky. There were continual modifications to all of the cars, not just his.

The hybrid technology they were using was so brilliant, so cutting-edge, and best of all, legal so far. The vehicle with the new tech had passed all their post-race required tests with flying colors. Racing was having a field day, pitting him against Maddux. Sport fans loved a rabid rivalry, and they got an authentic one with him and the Texan. It played well in the press, the juxtaposition of him against Maddux: the levelheaded, blond Brit versus the dark, hotheaded Texan. Even their goddamn names lent themselves shamelessly to the mockery. "Hawes and Bates—just a letter away from hates." The sport had even gained U.S. fans this season. Americans were late to F1, but according to his handler, they were as bad as the English in their addiction to tabloid journalism.

His phone vibrated, and he grabbed it. Cass. His heart leaped, and he struggled to quash his excitement. She'd left a long, halting apology in his voicemail before the race. And he'd almost forgiven her for misreading his character. How could she think he would use her, even for a second? Nothing had hurt more than that, except perhaps his father's betrayal.

She'd texted "Congrats."

He replied, "Going to party in five. See you there?"

"No. Media bloodthirsty. After?"

"Back in room by 11," he texted.

"See you there."

• • •

Two hours later he was desperate to escape. Knowing what was really happening with the car made the sponsor event unbearable. Between the veiled comments and the whispered conversations, it seemed everyone was onto this not-so-secret secret of the hybrid technology. He hoped to God the engineers could keep the damn thing together through the testing in Hockenheim.

He pushed the elevator button and entered. The doors were closing when a hand stopped them.

"Going somewhere?" Maddux stepped into the elevator.

Ronan's eyes narrowed.

"Can't stand the heat?"

"Talking crap again?" Ronan jabbed the button for his floor.

Maddux faced him. "How's this for crap? Your tech isn't ready for the big time, sport."

"Fuck off, loser."

"You're out of the turns pretty damn fast on that accelerator— quicker than any of us. You sure it won't fry you like it did Gregor in the preseason?

Ronan maintained his silence.

The elevator dinged its arrival at his floor. He shouldered his way past the American.

"Hold up," Maddux said, turning the corner and following him down the hall. Behind him the elevator dinged again.

Ronan stopped. "Don't you have anything better to do? Viv, perhaps?"

Maddux laughed. "You're still pissed about that? You didn't want her, but no one else can have her. Is that it? Chill, dude, it's nothing."

"She's only with you to cause me pain."

"It's worked pretty well," the other man said softly. "Anyway, it's over. "

"Do I look like I care?"

Maddux shrugged. "You're the one who brought her up. Whatever, man. Women. That's not what matters. What matters is what you're doing out there. For God's sake, this is the real deal, not a test track. You better be damn sure that your shit works, or you're putting us all in jeopardy. I don't plan to go out because I'm hit by a piece from your exploding car!"

"That's more like it. Always looking out for number one, aren't you? Meanwhile you're the real danger out there. A menace to all of us."

Ronan took two steps forward, putting himself inches from the scowling Maddux.

"Because I want to win?" Maddux's expression had gone from anger to confusion.

"Because you're inexperienced and reckless. You're either unaware or unconcerned with your own mortality. I plan to preserve my own."

"Then get them to take out that system, if you value your life. Even one of your engineers has been blabbing that it isn't ready."

"Bullshit," Ronan said. "Is that what you're here for? To warn me? You self-serving, manipulative arse. Sod off. You couldn't give a shit about me or the car. You're jealous and trying to wreck my head so you can win in Germany. Well, get this. You won't succeed."

Ronan turned on his heel, yanked the keycard out of his jacket pocket, and let himself into the room. He shrugged out of his jacket and tossed it on the sofa. A soft sound behind him sent him whipping around.

Cass. In the doorway, holding the door open.

She stood, pale and achingly beautiful.

His heart lurched and he took two hesitant steps toward her.

"Is it true?" she said, stepping forward, the door shutting silently behind her.

"Is what true?"

"Don't fuck with me, Ronan." Her voice was hoarse. "What I heard in the hall."

He sighed impatiently. "About Viv? That's over. Long over. I don't have feelings for her anymore. There's no room for them—not given the way I feel about you."

She stared uncomprehendingly. "Viv?"

"My ex—his—"

"I don't give a good goddamn about Vivienne McCloud." Her tone was dangerously low. "If you do have feelings for me, don't get killed out on that racetrack. If whatever you've got in your car is dangerous, to you and to the other drivers out there, don't race. Please, God, Ronan, don't put your life on the line out there for a fucking car race. I'm begging you. Please, I … care for you. I couldn't stand it." Her voice broke.

He rubbed his chin with a shaking hand. "It'll do."

Her mouth dropped open. "It'll *do*?" She shook her head. "Ronan."

"I know there's been talk, but it works. You saw that. It's just one more race."

Her body was trembling with barely suppressed emotion.

"Listen, Cass. It's not even my decision. These things are determined by the engineers, by Pantech."

His stomach flipped at her expression. She looked shattered.

"Maddux is right. You're not alone out there. You're putting everyone at risk."

His heart was racing now, faster than it did at the Prix today. "I know it sounds bad, especially to someone unfamiliar with Formula One, but—"

She took two steps backward, shaking her head. "My God," she said softly. "That you're complicit in something this dangerous—"

"Christ, Cass, I thought you understood. All I do is drive the goddamn car!"

She turned to walk out, then hesitated. "Remember the dune?" she said, her hand on the door handle.

"The dune?" What was she talking about?

"The dirt bikes. Remember how you felt when I went over that dune?"

"Oh. Yes."

She turned back to him, her expression stricken. "That. Times a thousand. If you don't value your life, Ronan, at least …" she opened the door, "at least know how much I value it."

She pulled the handle, walked through the door, and out of his life.

Chapter 18

Cass checked out of the hotel, rented a car, and drove through the night. Fifteen hours later she was home. Exhausted, unable to nap, she was ripe for a panic attack.

There was a knock at the door. Probably Andrea from next door, who had been keeping an eye on the place. Maybe Andrea could give her a ride to drop off the rental car.

Cass got up from the couch to answer it.

She'd come home to put her place on the market and give the proceeds to Mandy. It would go a long way to salving her conscience, or so she hoped. She had a lot to do before she called the Realtor. And she couldn't stop thinking about Ronan and his damned race. She flung open the door, the welcoming smile on her face faltering at the sight of a teenage boy on her doorstep.

"Hi," the boy said.

"Can I help you?"

He shifted awkwardly from one foot to the other, messing with the phone in his hand. "Cassidy Miller?"

"Yes?"

"Paul Garcia," the boy muttered.

She knew that name. All the blood drained from Cass's head as her blood pressure took a sudden severe drop. She grabbed the doorframe.

"You're Cassidy Miller, the pilot." More shuffling, still no eye contact.

"Yeah." She took a few deep breaths. She wasn't prepared for this—whatever he wanted, she couldn't give him.

He finally looked up, his eyes haunted, dark rings bruising the area under his eyes. "Can I talk to you?"

She pressed her lips together. It went against every instinct for self-preservation she had. She was raw and shaky, with nothing to distract her from her past—not alcohol and not Ronan. That fucking night. This fucking kid.

He waited, fiddling with his phone.

"Come on in," she finally said.

His shoulders sagged with relief.

She remembered his name, otherwise she wouldn't have recognized this skinny, pale, teen on her doorstep. When she'd last seen him, he'd been a bloodied mess on a backboard, with a white plastic immobilization device around his neck, hooked up to an intravenous line and an electrocardiograph.

She led the boy to the sofa opposite her and took a seat in the upright chair. He didn't even look old enough to drive, let alone drink.

"How'd you find me?"

He shook his phone. "Address, occupation, marital status—it's all here."

"Okaay," she said, slowly.

"To, uh, thank you. And to, uh, tell you I'm sorry."

At this unexpected announcement, grief welled up and expanded from her chest out to the nerve endings of her entire body. She took a shaky breath. "Well, thanks. I ... appreciate it."

He stared across the room.

This kid was really not comfortable with eye contact.

Cass glanced down. Oh. Maybe her thin tank top and pajama bottoms were making him uncomfortable.

She rose. "Get you anything?"

He looked hopeful. "Got any Supernova—the energy drink? Any energy drink actually, I live off of them these days since I don't sleep."

Cass pulled on a lightweight yellow fleece and filled a glass of water in the kitchen. She handed it to Paul and sat, curling her legs up under her.

"That stuff's no good you know, not for kids."

"I'm not a kid. Not anymore."

She met his tormented gaze directly.

"I'm sorry. I'm so sorry," he blurted out, as his face went from pale to mottled pink. "It's my fault … what happened. My parents paid a fine, and I've been doing community service, but it's not enough." He raised tear-filled eyes to Cass. "Will it ever be enough? I just want it to never have happened." He dashed his thin arm across his face, then hunched over, studying his hands in his lap.

Tears welled in Cass's eyes. "I don't know what to tell you, Paul. We all make mistakes. You're young, you're allowed to make mistakes. Is that what you want to hear?"

Paul shook his head.

"You were driving drunk, right?"

A nod.

"And you wrecked. It was our job to take you to where you could be treated. But you weren't the cause of *our* crash. I was."

"But if I hadn't gotten drunk that night and wrecked—"

There were no platitudes.

She sat stiffly, hands clenched, holding onto her self-control. She shook with the effort.

And now the boy was crying, great, gasping, half-man, half-boy sobs.

She got up and sat next to him on the sofa, instinctively putting one hand to his shoulder. "Paul?" It took a few minutes, but eventually the sobs died into hiccups. "Steve was a great guy. An amazing guy, actually, with a huge heart. And I think if he were here," she fought for control of her voice, "if he were here, he'd tell you don't drink and drive—ever again."

The kid nodded. "I won't."

"He'd tell you not to let the guilt define your life." Then she added softly, "Maybe the best we can do is make his sacrifice worthwhile."

After a few moments of letting him cry, Cass patted him firmly on the back. It was time for both of them to stop floundering. "I really appreciate you searching me out. I'll let the medic's family know how you feel, okay?"

His shoulders slumped with relief. He gave her an awkward hug, and she walked him to the door. He shuffled down the path and gave her a farewell wave before climbing in his battered Toyota and driving away.

Could it be that simple?

Steve had cared about her. Cared about all his crew. He'd never want her to spend her life wallowing in guilt. Calm certainty and a kind of peace crept through her. It was time to move on, figure out where to go from here. Figure out how to forgive herself. Figure out how to fly again. And she couldn't do it alone. What Anderson and Ronan had hinted at was very true. In a daze, she walked over to her purse and fished out the cell phone number of the psychiatrist that Julie had talked to after the accident who specialized in post-traumatic stress disorder.

She dialed the number with trembling fingers.

Chapter 19

His race was in Germany in five days.

Cassidy paced the waiting room of the psychiatrist's office. She was coming out of her skin. Not over her past, for once, but over Ronan and his stupid car. Apparently Ronan and Maddux had a shoving match at the track as they exited their vehicles after a test drive in Germany. Crew members had rushed in to separate them. The YouTube video of that little spat had a million hits and counting. The press was breathless about the rivalry, and Formula One PR was in heaven exploiting it. Today's *Race Fan Magazine* headline had been "Maddux Baits Hawes." And this Vivienne McCloud creature in her slinky, black dresses moping about in the tabloids like a poor man's Audrey Hepburn in her giant hats and sunglasses, only added to the frenzy. She played the role of femme fatale to perfection, managing to get caught by photo-stalkers as she went into retail-therapy mode all over London.

They'd practically had a seizure this morning when she got on a flight to Germany. Was she headed to make up with Ronan? Or his archrival Maddux? Or, the cynic in Cass thought, paid by the F1 PR firm to drum up interest in the final race? After everything that went down in Texas, she refused to believe he had rekindled things with Vivienne. She staunchly suppressed the tiny, niggling doubt.

Most of the time, Cass was thankful for Vivienne McCloud. It should be her the media was stalking. Cassidy Miller, American woman helicopter pilot, killer, and drunken occupant of Hawes's vehicle in Texas, had vanished from their radar. She pushed her hair out of her eyes, stuffing it into a ponytail.

"Cass?"

Dr. Ames pushed open the door, and Cass marched in.

"I sense you're a bit agitated today. Are you rethinking the medication we talked about?"

"No. I'm—It's not that. I think the exposure therapy is helping. I'm hoarse from talking about what happened that night, to you, to Julie, to Anderson, and Jim, and my mom. I'm getting sick of hearing myself talk about it. And I haven't had nightmares since I started seeing you last week. For once I'm not obsessing over the accident. My—"

He leaned forward in his chair and gestured to the couch. "Sit. Please."

Cass tossed herself onto the beige loveseat with a grunt.

"The man I … my … Ronan Hawes's race is just days away. He's taking a huge risk. His car has been modified, and it's a modification that makes it less safe. It's the reason we broke up."

"You broke up over a car part?" The psychiatrist's voice rose half an octave.

"No, over the risk … Never mind."

"It's a risky occupation. How does it make you feel, caring for someone who puts his life on the line every week?"

"That part I get. That part I can accept. The problem is that the car's not safe, and it's not just his life at stake. There are other drivers out on that track who could be hurt or killed if something were to happen."

"I can see where a high level of risk brings up some issues for you," he said calmly.

"What? For me?" she said. "Please. Flying EMS is the one of the riskiest occupations out there. I accept that he's willing to risk his life for his job. How could I have a quarrel with that?"

"Because it causes you more anxiety."

"Okay, yeah. It is hard to watch. At first it was fun, thrilling. But now that I … I love him, it's terrifying," she admitted. "But it's what he does, part of who he is. I don't believe in people giving up what they love for someone else. And he wouldn't either. What

I can't accept is that he would race a car that's not safe. And it makes me angry. Not just that he might be injured or killed, but that he might kill someone else in the name of speed."

"Ah." He scribbled on his notepad. "Listen to what you're saying. You understand him putting his life at stake, the way you do for your job, but risking the life of others is unacceptable to you after your experience." He scribbled something in the journal next to him.

She hated when he made notes. She hated it more when he tracked everything back to her accident. This wasn't about that. "You think I'm wrong?" she said.

"I think his situation and the choices he's making are creating conflict because you're having trouble separating what he's doing with your accident and the repercussions."

"I don't think so."

"So if you were Ronan, what would you do?"

"Me?" Cass asked. "I wouldn't race with parts that weren't fully vetted and functioning properly. I'm a pilot. If you get indicators telling you an engine or a part is on the fritz, you don't fly. Period."

"And he's told you that's what's happening?"

"Not in so many words. But it *was* a problem. And I've heard—" What had she heard? Rumors. Had Ronan actually said the new technology wasn't working properly? He'd said, "It'll do." Maybe this was all sour grapes fueled by the other teams because he was faster than anyone else and privy to a better, faster car. No. He was stressed about it. But wouldn't he be stressed about the final race, the pressure, and the changes to the car anyway? Was this a given in racing?

Maybe it came down to trust. She hadn't been so great at that lately.

"Let's get back to your feelings about flying and your career."

...

Ronan ground his teeth together and hung up the phone. Jesus. It would be a miracle if he could get his head together for the race tomorrow. He was obsessing. And the hell of it was, he didn't disagree with her. She'd said all the things he initially said to Martin. But it *was* just one more race. And most of the time the damn car did phenomenally well with the new system. If only they could figure out what had put it out of sorts toward the end of the race in Texas. If only Cassidy understood the sport. Or understand why he was willing to take these risks. She was an idealist. It was probably what drew her to flying sick people around in the first place. Idealism didn't fare well in the cold, hard world of F1 that he inhabited. Yet he accepted her. Damn it, he loved her. Her feelings couldn't possibly be as strong if she ran at the first hint of trouble.

But God, he'd do anything for her.

He rubbed his chest. It wasn't possible for his heart to actually ache, but it did. When she had walked out of his hotel room in Texas, everything had fallen apart.

He'd certainly never felt this desperate, all-consuming bleakness. Him. At the top of his game, poised to win the championship. What he'd been planning for, dreaming of, for years couldn't overcome the hollow emptiness. She'd managed to strip him of his protective outer layer and had left him raw and emotionally exposed. She'd found the part of him that he kept separate, the part he'd never opened to anyone, until her. He had no idea what to do with this almost violent desperation to be with her. To hold her when nightmares woke her. He couldn't protect her from the fallout from her past, but at least he had been there for a little while.

He hoped Anderson or someone was there for her, but God, he'd do anything to have her back.

There was a knock at the door.

Cass?

His heart leaped, and he strode to the door and flung it open.

Bloody hell.

"Dad!"

The man looked old. Frail, with a pasty complexion. Prison pallor, no doubt. Still, there was a lot of life behind those wicked, bright blue eyes. And Ronan felt ... nothing. All those years he'd spent practicing speeches about ethics and humiliation. All the rage and shame. Here was the man responsible for all those feelings, and the only thing Ronan felt was emptiness?

He stared at his father out in the hallway, still waiting for a delayed reaction, an avalanche of suppressed feelings. But nothing came. .

"They released me on Thursday, son. I tried to get a ticket to the track from your team, but they advised me it wouldn't be the best thing to be seen with you." He wrung his hands "The press doesn't need another scandal this week. That's what they're saying."

"Another scandal?"

"That matter with the ... the arrest?"

Ronan sighed. "There was no arrest."

"Ah well, you know the American papers—big on their stories, not so big on their facts."

"It was nothing," he said, wearily. It was too late to kill whoever had leaked that story. Maddux, no doubt.

"Well, I saw it on the telly in the pub—they pulled you over with spirits on you. That's not like you, son. But the speeding? That I can believe." He grinned. "Occupational hazard, eh?"

Ronan rubbed his forehead. God. This was all he needed.

"I've a sponsor dinner now. Take a seat. I need to change. Be back in a moment."

Ronan closed the doors to his room, leaving his father perched on the couch in the sitting room in his ill-fitting suit.

He went to the closet and pulled out his freshly pressed custom made Armani suit and shirt. He felt slightly ill as he did up the buttons. His fingers fumbled as they tied his blue tie, and it took twice as long as usual. His mind was blank with anger. Harry had taken the decision away from him as usual and just shown up on the worst possible night. It had been too much to hope that he'd just lay low in the British countryside after his release. No, he had to come charging across the channel, however the hell he managed to get past border controls, and shove his nose where it was least wanted.

Tucking the phone in his jacket pocket, he flung open the doors to the suite.

His father's face lit up. "Son." The man pulled a handkerchief from his pocket. "Look at you," he whispered.

Ronan took the straight-backed chair across from the old man. "Why are you here?"

"To see you, of course."

The silence lengthened, becoming uncomfortable. Ronan shifted on the chair.

Harry dabbed his eyes with the white square. "I'm just so proud."

The anger was dissipating now; chagrin and compassion were taking its place. The man had always believed in him. Even as a child. There'd been many moments when he'd uttered those words to a little boy. He was generous with praise when it was due.

"I always knew you were capable of it. And I'm going to make you proud, too, son. I still have a few friends willing to back me." He looked down, twisting the handkerchief. "That's to say, as long as you're behind me, they are."

Ronan's spine straightened. "What?"

"As long as you believe in me—"

"Back you?"

"Yes, these people understand my situation."

Ronan leaned forward. "What situation? You defrauded thousands of people."

"No, no, that's where you're wrong. I know you don't understand the financials, the market. You see, I *had* the money invested, but the market turned." The liver-spotted hands were strangling the white cloth.

Ronan folded his arms across his chest. "I read the files, Harry, I read the court documents."

"Oh, yes, the court documents." Harry shook his head. "They needed someone to blame when the pensioners lost money. But if the market hadn't turned the way it did, well, they'd have made their investment and then some."

My God. He hadn't changed a bit.

"So, I have new clients, but, well, I don't have much start-up capital. But with you behind me—"

"So it's my money, my name, you want to capitalize on now?"

His father's held tilted, his blue eyes intent. "I know Formula One has kept you from me. I know that my reputation—well, I understand F1 needed to keep up appearances. Especially after those pensioners went to the press. But, son, just being seen with you—"

"I don't believe this. I don't believe you would come here—"

"Who put you here?" Harry asked, tone deceptively soft. "Who put you in this suite, in that fancy suit?"

"I put myself here, Harry."

His father shook his head. "You didn't do it alone, did you? And I'm not asking for much."

"You'll get nothing from me." Ronan stood, hands clenched into fists by his side. "I've spent the past five years funneling money, trying to make amends to the people you stole from. I'll be damned if I give you the chance to steal again."

Harry sprang forward in his seat. "You *what?*"

Ronan took a few paces around the room, never moving his eyes off his father's face. "One quarter of my income each year goes into a fund to pay restitution to the people you stole from."

In one shaky maneuver, his father stood, his face no longer pale. Instead, it was mottled with rage. "Those people? They took a gamble, and they lost, and you've been giving them *money*?"

Ronan laughed, but it was bitter. "Yes. And you," he strode to the door and opened it, "have overstayed your welcome."

"So holier-than-thou," his father hissed from the threshold. "Such a saint of a son that I have," he sneered. "When you're as likely as me to be bending and twisting the rules."

Ronan recoiled.

"At least that's what they're saying, my boy. Anything to win. You got that from me." His father dropped his hand, releasing the door and backed away as Ronan stood. Frozen.

He felt the blood drain from his face. Is this what he'd turned into? A man willing to do whatever it took? Risk his life and those of everyone else out there on the circuit for a shot at a win? When he'd already lost the one thing that mattered?

Ronan all but pushed his father out the door. He walked to the bed, sat down, and pulled out his phone.

• • •

"Then you need to find yourself another driver," Ronan said, calmly.

"What? Have you lost your bloody mind? The race is tomorrow!" Martin sputtered.

"Right. And if you don't take out that hybrid technology and put in the authorized one, you'll be needing to replace me for the race."

Martin smiled slyly. "You won't do it."

Ronan's blood pounded in his ears, but he kept his face expressionless. "Watch me."

He turned on his heel. Good thing he hadn't already suited up for the practice. It was out of his hands now.

Martin called after him. "Wait. Ronan."

He stopped in his tracks. The other man trotted up, red-faced and scowling. "Okay, we'll change it out."

Ronan nodded.

Martin moved closer and pointed at Ronan's chest, his thin lips white with fury. "But know this, you'll be looking for another ride next season—no matter what happens tomorrow."

"You better believe it," Ronan said, standing his ground. "I take that risk out there. And why do I take it? Because I've faith in my ability to drive that car to its limits, yes. But also because I've one hundred percent faith in that team you've assembled. I've chosen this life and these risks. Call me arrogant, fine. I'm arrogant. It takes arrogance to get out there and risk your life, health, and safety for a race. But it's not just me out there. This is no test track. No driver would," he amended, "no driver should take those kinds of risks—knowing the modification isn't ready. When the car is telling me that there are problems, I choose to listen."

Martin walked away, stiff with rage.

Ronan had no faith that management would do it. He'd have to rely on Benny to organize it somehow. Ronan stood scowling at the garages for several minutes. So he'd managed to stay true to his ethics, just barely, yet there was still a gaping hole.

Cass.

If he'd only found his wobbly scruples a day or two earlier. But she was finished with him, and who could blame her? Granted, F1 and its "modifications" frequently blurred the lines, and safety was relative in this business, but she didn't believe in relativism, in smudging the lines, under any circumstances. Her moral vision was twenty-twenty.

He'd thought her to be overreacting when she'd approached him—her past experiences and her idealism mucking up the waters with this issue. But it was he who had the problem. He and many others in this business. It had taken that scoundrel of a father for him to see clearly. The risk wasn't worth it.

Of course, the trick would be winning tomorrow. Hockenheim favored the American—conditions would be miserable. Ronan fished out his lucky round pebble and threw it across the tarmac.

Two bounces.

"*Scheisse.*"

•••

"Thanks for fetching me, Anderson. I could've taken the train or rented a car."

Her father held her at arm's length and examined her. "You look good, Cass." His tone registered surprise.

She let out a shaky laugh and opened the door of his rented Audi A8. "Do I? That's hard to believe after a cross-country then a transatlantic flight."

"How did it go?" Anderson asked, as they buckled their seat belts.

"I managed without the in-flight drinks. I have a prescription, but I didn't need it. We've worked on some things that seem to be helping. I white-knuckled it a bit through some turbulence, but everyone else seemed to be doing pretty much the same thing."

He squeezed her shoulders. "You're better. You certainly look more relaxed." He started the Audi.

"I'm seeing a psychiatrist," she admitted. "Post-traumatic stress disorder is my official diagnosis."

"Damn. I'm sorry, love. And?"

"I have a ways to go. Though, I've been able to think of little but Ronan the last few days."

Anderson shot her a look. "He didn't drive this morning."

Her eyes widened. "What?"

"No. We were told the car was having issues. He'll drive later today though. He needs to."

"What's going on?"

"No one knows. The Pantech owner has been all smiles and good cheer, anticipating a championship. Haven't seen Ronan, but that's not unusual. You know they go into hibernation before the big race. You don't want to drop your things at the hotel?"

She patted her overnight bag on her lap. "Nah. I packed light.

• • •

It was hard to believe just weeks ago she'd watched him race with excitement. Nervous excitement, granted. But excitement all the same.

Now that she'd finally acknowledged her feelings for him, finally accepted how much she loved and needed him in her life, watching him strap himself into a rocket led her to a whole different universe of fear.

Feeling the tension radiating from her, Anderson laid a hand over hers clasped in her lap.

"You okay?"

She gave him what she hoped passed for a smile, but judging by his concerned expression, she hadn't succeeded.

"It's difficult to watch, I imagine."

She nodded, scanning the brightly colored cars, the men and women in safety gear making final checks.

"He's the best," Anderson said quietly. "One of the most experienced drivers in the pack—"

"Yeah? It doesn't help to know that. Anything could happen."

•••

Ronan gazed out at the shimmering sea of German fans. The press was still slinking away from Maddux's tour bus, where the Texan, with a bleached-teeth smile plastered on his face, had been handing out the cans of Supernova to adoring fans an hour ago. Maddux's very Americanness made him something of a novelty here in Europe. No American had ever won the Hockenheimring circuit, and no doubt he was dying to be the first. Literally dying if necessary. Ronan turned sharply and started getting his own gear ready.

When it came down to it, man against man, who was the better driver? That's what the world really wanted to know. That's what he wanted to know.

The circuit was dry. Maddux had zero natural advantage here, but the man was in pole position after the qualifiers. Ronan was in top form. He could do this. The past evenings had been spent alone working out at the gym, then sitting on his bedroom floor beside his laptop re-enacting the tight curves and the optimal gear changes, until he decided that he was maybe losing it.

He slammed his helmet on despite the blistering headache. He'd resisted painkillers; they'd only blunt his reactions. It would be over soon, and then he could rest for the remainder of his life if he wanted to.

Adrenaline obliterated all those weaknesses when he jetted off the starting line. His eyes riveted to the black and orange of Maddux's vehicle. It was clear this would be a duel, and the others would trail away.

As expected, a dangerous scuffle broke out between the two drivers the second the starting lights flashed on. Ronan got the lead, and he whooped for joy. Coming out of the bend on lap sixty-six, he fought for vision, the sun blinding him while his migraine flashed red at the sides of his eye sockets. An orange car zoomed past. Maddux. Ronan froze in disbelief for an awful moment suspended in time. Then he came to and cursed loudly, not giving a damn who heard. The headphones squawked with his team's own pandemonium, cursing too and yelling out pointless advice, leaving Ronan tempted to slam the audio off. He ignored it all and concentrated on getting the lead back. There were two positions on the circuit where it was possible, between the Nordkurve and the Sudkurve, and four more laps in which to realistically achieve it. He just needed this last pit stop first.

• • •

"Would you do it, Dad?"

His gaze never left the racetrack. "I'm no saint, Cass. My company has put people's lives at stake, and people have been killed on rigs. Safety measures aren't the primary concern in my business. Profit is.

"That's not what I asked."

"I'd like to think I wouldn't jeopardize my safety or the safety of others for a championship. But it's easy for me to say that, sitting up here on my high horse."

"Huh," he said, brow furrowed.

"Huh?"

"He's quick but, he doesn't seem to be coming out of the turns the way he was in Texas. Or at the prelims."

She scooted to the edge of her seat, sparing her father a glance as Ronan's vehicle sped down the track. She raised her binoculars as he hit the next turn.

"Will that change anything?" Anderson asked.

Would it?

I don't know.

She groaned. "Anderson, I'm trying to … to work it out in my head. I'm here because … because I couldn't bear to watch from

5,000 miles away. I didn't want him to race alone. I want to be here in case, in case things go wrong. In case he needs me. I need to be there for him the way he's been there for me."

Her eyes burned as the race went on endlessly, coming out of her skin with anxiety. She tried the breathing exercises she'd been taught. She held Anderson's hand.

If something happens out there, my heart will never recover.

...

There'd be no more pit stops now. It was driver against driver. On lap seventy, Ronan saw his chance to out-accelerate Maddux at the start of the hill, but mindful of the barriers further up, he had to hang back. A millisecond earlier and he'd have done it, but a millisecond later, he'd have crashed. He clenched his teeth. Next lap … next lap. The pressure of his entire life was crushing his skull, squeezing the sweat from every pore. This is what a fight to the death meant, but now he knew he didn't want to die. Cass's blue silk underwear he'd stuffed inside his suit that was pressing against his heart. Not for luck—no, for something altogether more powerful.

His migraine lifted, and a calm serenity enveloped his tortured synapses like a cooling balm. He knew how to do this. He knew how to do this without risking his life or anyone else's. It was a matter of pure skill and timing. He just had to stay focused and get that millisecond right.

Two laps later, it was there. The moment. He slammed down the accelerator at the base of the hill and zoomed past Maddux's orange car. He slowed down as necessary for the Nordkurve, and then fled through, accelerating before hitting the Sudkurve. Would Maddux have slowed down enough on the bend after being overtaken? Ronan strained to hear what the team was telling him on the audio. All he could hear was the white noise of shouting.

"He swerved! Go for it you, bastard," Benny was yelling. "Maddux has gone bananas. He'll kill himself on the hairpin!"

Ronan's breath came in short puffs. With Maddux only one inch behind, he'd have a chance to catch up coming around the hairpin, into the sun. Not his favorite part. He blinked the sweat from his eyes and clenched his fingers, his gut, and his soul in preparation for the final mile. Blinded or not, he'd drive through using instinct only and make it … around the Nordkurve again … to the finish line.

A chequered flag registered in the periphery of his vision. That meant someone had won. But who? Maddux's car was decelerating beside his. Too close to tell. Through the screams of confusion from his team, he couldn't make out who'd gotten the edge. But now he just felt … sheer, utter relief. He'd wanted this peace for so long. He yearned for fresh air, coolness, quiet, softness. A new start. Her.

"Fuck it anyway," Benny's gravelly voice, came through the headset, cutting through the noise. His tone said it all. He'd lost. The team had lost. Maddux had won by the fraction of a hair, measured with über-precise German timing equipment.

•••

He spotted her in the crowd. Unbelievable really, considering the throngs of people surrounding the podium. She and Anderson had been making their way down the grandstand—Anderson Miller slowed by glad-handing. His spirits lifted. She wouldn't be here if she didn't care.

Benny gave his shoulder a punch. "Regrets?"

A smile spread across his face as he met his engineer's concerned gaze. "None whatsoever. Listen, Benny, chin up. I appreciate what you did for me. Despite the outcome. You have to believe that."

Benny nodded, chewing his gum slowly. "Could be you up there though." He indicated the area where Maddux stood, surrounded by an ever-growing crowd of sponsors and supporters and teammates. Ronan spared the Texan a glance, then he turned back to study the crowd, searching and finding Cassidy Miller. "Mmm hmm."

"Ronan?"

"Things to do, Benny," he said, moving forward, handing his helmet to the startled gray-haired man.

"Wait, Ronan, the podium—"

But he barely heard him. He was rushing through the frenzied crowd, searching out his brunette.

Adrenaline sang through his system. He would've sworn he'd expended all of it during the race.

He fought his way through a crowd of Germans shouting "*Bravo!*" "*Gut gemacht,*" "*nächstes Jahr, gel?*" Well done, next year again, eh?

And then there she was—shocked, if the look on her face was anything to go by. He swiped a hand across his face She stood, staring, for half a second. Time stretched painfully as he tried to read her.

Then she took a half step forward, her searching gaze never leaving his, and leaped into his arms.

He staggered backward, finding his balance. He lowered his head to her upturned mouth and kissed her with all the desperation, all the pent up passion as if had been months, years instead of days. She tasted of mint and oranges, her tongue searching out, finding his and tangling. Everything faded out. The noise, the crowd, her father—

He lifted his head, reluctantly releasing her lips but maintaining his grip on her shoulders.

"Cass," he said shakily, gathering her into his body.

She gripped him, hard.

He pushed her away, scanning her face. "You all right?"

"Fine." Her voice was breathless, her face, radiant. "You?"

He nodded.

"I'm sorry," she whispered.

"For what?" He half laughed. "You were right."

"Yes, but you didn't win."

Her father, the crowds, the photographers who had followed him in his desperate search—all of them be damned.

He lowered his head and whispered against her smiling mouth, "Oh yes, I bloody well did."

Epilogue

"Ready?"

"As I'll ever be," Ronan responded into his microphone. She could almost hear him grinning through that calm voice, that accent purring through her headphones.

It had taken months of patience and therapy, but she was back to manning the cockpit.

Her license hadn't been suspended by the FAA, and thanks to Anderson's efforts, Nautilus had given her a short-term oil and gas contract as second-in-command of an S-92 helicopter in the North Sea region—some of the most challenging weather for flying in the world. Nepotism and trial by fire. But the pilot she was paired with had been flying those rough conditions for a dozen years. He had told her stories of fog and hard landings and rogue waves that had made her stomach churn. Her confidence had increased with each flight, and they'd spent the first weeks ferrying equipment instead of roughnecks, which was a blessing.

Flying over the North Sea was miserable, and the living quarters weren't much better on a headland that jutted into the ocean. It wasn't the job she loved—EMS would always be unbeatable in that category—but at least she was back in the cockpit, two weeks flying, two weeks off with Ronan.

He'd shown her his favorite places all over London, all over Europe.

She'd been seeing a therapist during her time off in London who specialized in PTSD cases, and whose clients were mostly veterans. The nightmares still came, but they were few and far between, and Cass hadn't had a drop to drink since that infamous night in Texas.

She'd used some of her trust fund to settle with Mandy Morten. Mandy was still pursuing legal action against both her and EvacuAir. But Cass's guilt and sorrow had abated, and she no longer had to sacrifice her happiness because of what had happened that night.

And then Ronan had surprised her with this trip back to Arizona and a chance to see her family before his racing season restarted. There were still plenty of issues to hammer out—she had no idea where she'd fly when this Nautilus contract was up. Ronan wanted her on the road with him, but she wasn't going to follow him around like some track groupie.

There were tour company contracts, executive travel contracts, fire contracts—anything but EMS. She might eventually go back, but she would trust her gut on that one, and her gut still heaved at the idea of on-scene night calls. Contracting allowed tremendous flexibility—she and Ronan would find ways to be together.

She moved her left hand to the collective, and they were up, hovering weightlessly above the concrete surface of the helipad. This little Robinson 44 hadn't been cheap to rent from the flight school, but Mr. Extravagant wanted to take a tour, and she knew just the place to take him: a little lake eighty miles from the airport, practically in her parents' backyard. She had a basket of food, a blanket, and condoms. She'd even managed to borrow a beat-up pickup at the tiny airport to take them over to the water.

She glanced over at her passenger. Ronan was sitting forward in his seat, marveling at the view out the window.

"Amazing," he said softly, so softly she could barely hear him in her headphones over the rotors.

She nodded, grinning. This place was beautiful. It was home. But she no longer felt like she'd been banished from paradise. Living overseas with Ronan was just a different kind of perfect.

She crested the mountain. Only one boat was out on the water, barely a ripple in the surface. A motorboat, exactly the kind that

Piero's nephew had used to pick them up sopping wet back in Venice.

Ronan leaned forward, pointing at it. "You know—"

"Oh yes, I remember," she said, flashing him a grin. "I think we're safer up here than in the water, don't you?"

* * *

Mid-afternoon Cass packed up their things, while Ronan fiddled around with his duffel bag. "So, Cass? I have news." He held a familiar neon orange ball cap by the bill. Cass stepped closer. "Is that a Supernova cap?"

His nod was sheepish. "Maddux sent it."

"Maddux? Did you bring it here to pitch it in the lake?" she asked hopefully.

"He sent it as a gesture of goodwill. I … I signed with them. You're looking at Supernova's newest driver."

She'd known it was a possibility, of course. As the season approached, he needed a ride. His desperation recently had been palpable.

"Did they give Maddux the boot then?"

"Uh … no. He's my teammate."

Cass cocked her head. "I love you, Ronan, but I'm not sure I can root for Supernova, and I hope you don't expect me to drink that stuff," she teased.

"Uh, Cass?"

"Yeah?" She popped the top on the cooler.

"That's not all." He shook the cap at her.

"Am I supposed to put it on or something—oh. Wait. What's this?" A square black object in the bottom of the cap nearly fell out into her hand.

Her heart thudded to a halt, then picked up at triple normal speed.

He smiled, took a knee and gave her the grin that had turned half the female population in the U.K. into rabid F1 racing fans.

"Cassidy Miller, will you marry me?"

She covered her mouth with a hand. Her vocal cords had seized up, so she managed a nod.

He reached for her hand, and she could see his weren't steady either.

"What are we doing?" she whispered.

"I don't just love you, Cass. I don't think I can live without you. Just open it, would you?

She tossed the cap aside, opened the box, and withdrew a perfect solitaire flanked by sapphires.

A watery giggle escaped her.

His eyes narrowed. "What? The blue? It reminds me of your eyes," he said, defensively thrusting the ring onto her finger.

She pulled him up by the shoulders. "I love you. You and your damned luck."

More from This Author
(From *Spiraling* by Rachel Cross)

An odd snapping sensation and a rush of slick heat accompanied his final thrust. A thrust that seated him balls deep in disaster. Shane Marx retracted his hips, removed his hands from the smooth, firm ass and took two stumbling steps away from the woman on her hands and knees on the edge of the bed. Too late. He stared down in horror at the remnants of the condom, still attached at the base, a wide tear splitting the tip.

Motherfucker.

The woman's body trembled from the effects of his exertions.

His heart rate ratcheted up. "Uh." He racked his brain for a name. Nope. Nothing. Given how swiftly things proceeded at the club, he wasn't sure they'd exchanged that information. She knew who he was, and after thirty minutes of foreplay in the guise of dancing, she'd been eager to get him back to her place.

"We may have a problem," he said.

The woman belly flopped onto floral sheets, then rolled over with a satisfied groan. She looked at him, her face slack with the remnants of pleasure and fatigue, mascara smeared almost to her cheeks. She pushed tangled blonde hair off her damp face. "What?"

Following his gaze she spotted the ruined condom and her eyes widened. Her hand investigated the apex of her thighs and she giggled.

He clenched his teeth.

"Oh." Her smile was coy. "You don't have to worry. I'm clean."

"Yeah? That's good. Me too." But that wasn't his greatest concern, and from the calculating gleam in her eye, she knew it.

He pressed his palm to his forehead as fears of paternity suits, child-custody hearings, and tabloid photos throbbed to life.

What were the odds? Slim to maybe? He had never, ever had a condom failure. TruAchord would have been dead on arrival if he or any of his boy-band mates had been hit with a paternity suit back in the day. Years later he was still neurotic about using them.

Shane backed up until he was in the attached bathroom. He peeled off and flushed the condom. "Are you on the pill or anything?" he called out. When he came back into the room she was kneeling on the bed, holding up her iPhone to take a picture of him. He covered himself with both hands, took two strides forward, and wrested the phone from her grasp. He flipped through her photos, deleting the fuzzy one she'd taken as his heart thundered in his chest.

"Hey!"

He glared at her. "So not cool."

His agent would have a seizure if more naked photos emerged. The one some twit sent out last month had been bad enough. "Good God, Shane! Who wants to see a full frontal of you *sleeping*? At least the quarterbacks and politicians have the decency to get photos of their *erections*. Don't get me wrong, we should count ourselves lucky you're a show-er and not a grower, but this is a disaster! I'm having a hell of a time passing this off as a Photoshop job."

Apparently there was such a thing as bad publicity, and that picture had killed his audition for a lead in the latest Sparks film. No matter. He was done being typecast as the guy with issues in all that chick-flick crap. Maybe that photo would put him in consideration for a grittier role, but two? Two photos would indicate he had a problem. He held her phone while he slipped on his jeans. He pocketed it, and then checked his pants for wallet, keys, and his phone. Two steps across matted beige carpeting took him to the doorway where he spared her a glance.

She frowned at him from where she stood, naked beside the bed, one hand on a curvaceous hip, the other stroking through highlighted extensions. She spent way too much time in the tanning booth. The florescent light from the bathroom gave her skin a terracotta glow.

Revulsion surged through him.

"Are you on the pill or not?" he repeated.

"No."

"Is there something you can take? You know, so there aren't any unwanted repercussions?"

She shrugged. "Probably."

"Do you want me to set something up?" Should he offer her money or would that piss her off?

"I'll take care of it," she assured him, breaking eye contact.

His gut clenched. There wasn't much he could do at four in the morning. Or anytime for that matter. It wasn't as though he could march her to the pharmacy or a doctor's office or wherever.

Shane glanced around the room for clues to the woman's psyche. Neat, and decorated with some flair—though the bureau and nightstand screamed thrift store special. Poor, not slovenly.

It was always the same. The initial thrill, diminishing interest as things progressed to the point of no return, and the emptiness and awkwardness after. Now fear had entered the equation.

"Will you give me back my goddamn phone?" she said, extending a hand.

Shane turned his back on her and hustled through the apartment. He pulled a wad of bills from his money clip and chucked them along with her phone in the vicinity of the stained sofa. He made his way down the stairs of the second story garden apartment and onto the street. He'd been so distracted by her head bobbing in his lap in the back seat of the taxi he hadn't the faintest idea where he was. His phone showed him standing smack in the middle of Brantley, eight miles and several worlds away from his Santa Monica neighborhood. He turned west and started his jog of shame home.

For more books by Rachel Cross, also check out:

Rock Her

Rock Him

And from Ashlinn Craven:

Maybe Baby

In the mood for more Crimson Romance?
Check out *Marrying the Wrong Man* by Elley Arden at
CrimsonRomance.com.

www.ingramcontent.com/pod-product-compliance
Lightning Source LLC
Chambersburg PA
CBHW010309100726
47905CB00011B/3269

9 781440 581854